PRAISE FOR *ELSEWHERE, CALIFO*

"In this debut novel, Johnson brilliantly knits the du[...] gether, maintaining a dynamic balance between nimble language and rowdy, vulnerable characters. The real achievement is the honest, compassionate, and unflinching willingness to honor teenage struggles for identity, confidence, and love while listening to Led Zeppelin and rooting for the Dodgers." —*Publishers Weekly*, Starred Review

"Avery's evolution —a black woman trying to claim her place —is as heartbreaking as it is humorous, powerful as it is poignant, because Johnson so assertively confronts those complexities."
—Lynell George, *Los Angeles Times*

"Beautifully wrought. A contemporary Bildungsroman with a wise and winning heroine at its heart." —T.C. Boyle

"Dana Johnson's *Elsewhere, California* is a clear-eyed jam on class, race, and love; sassy yet searing." —Oscar Hijuelos

"I am in love with a woman named Avery and I have only heard her voice. She exists in these pages, radiates from them. Dana Johnson weaves the complex strings of modern identity into a tapestry that is both familiar yet refreshingly new." —Mat Johnson, author of *Pym*

"Dana Johnson's extraordinary novel offers an arresting vision of black female identity that transcends color and class even as it reveals its continuing power in our lives. The main character, Avery, is everything at once: struggling and middle-class, black and not-quite-black-enough, sexually invisible and sexually exoticized. Avery is about as complex and compelling a heroine as I've read recently, and Elsewhere, California is a luminous, funny, and poignant tale that speaks directly to a whole generation raised in a state of cultural confusion."
—Danzy Senna, author of *Caucasia*

"I love listening to Avery talk about anything and everything, from the Dodgers to the art world to neighborhood negotiations to certain brands of shorts. Here is a character with an intensely engaging voice, surrounded by an equally riveting cast, all created by a writer who knows how to make words and people sparkle on the page."
—Aimee Bender, author of *The Color Master*

"Reading Elsewhere, California, Dana Johnson's luminous, intelligent, linguistically dexterous first novel about growing up in Southern California, made me understand exponentially more about my own state, my own growing up, and the private lives of families in the homes all around me. An impressive, inspiring debut!"

—Michelle Huneven, author of *Off Course*

PRAISE FOR *BREAK ANY WOMAN DOWN*

"Dana Johnson's collection of stories contains so many wonderful women. Living, breathing, making a million mistakes, but you understand every one of them. Sometimes you think your heart will burst, but the pain is illustrated with depth, clarity, and beauty."

—Victor LaValle, author of Big Machine and *The Ecstatic*

"This is an exciting and gorgeous literary debut."

—Jonathan Ames, author of *The Extra Man*

"You can hear Johnson's voices ringing long after you put the stories down…No character could stay a stranger long in this writer's hands."

—*Los Angeles Times*

"[A] sometimes comical read…Johnson's stories are ultimately bound by the human desire to find a place…to fit in."

—*USA Today*

"Deftly achieves both art and amusement…Johnson's ability to coax the heart as much as the mind…marks the author as a storyteller at her most potent."

—*Seattle Weekly*

"Whether it's an awkward sixth grader with a crush, a pair of brazen Iranian sisters, or a male porno star who bakes a mean ziti, Dana Johnson's characters breathe authenticity. Johnson has got range and she's got depth. A remarkable new voice has emerged."

—Dalton Conley, author of *Honky*

"Rich, unhurried layering showcases [Johnson's] larger themes…Both hip and elegant, these assured stories…simmer and resonate."

—*Publishers Weekly*

IN THE NOT QUITE DARK

IN THE NOT QUITE DARK

{ stories }

Dana Johnson

COUNTERPOINT • BERKELEY, CALIFORNIA

Library of Congress Cataloging-in-Publication Data is Available

Names: Johnson, Dana, 1967- author.
Title: In the not quite dark : stories / Dana Johnson.
Description: Berkeley : Counterpoint, [2016]
Identifiers: LCCN 2015046441 | ISBN 9781619027329 (softcover)
Subjects: | BISAC: FICTION / Short Stories (single author).
Classification: LCC PS3610.O33 A6 2016 | DDC 813/.6--dc23
LC record available at http://lccn.loc.gov/2015046441

Cover design by Kelly Winton
Interior design by Neuwirth & Associates

ISBN 978-1-61902-732-9

Counterpoint
2560 Ninth Street, Suite 318
Berkeley, CA 94710
www.counterpointpress.com

Printed in the United States of America
Distributed by Publishers Group West

10 9 8 7 6 5 4 3 2 1

CONTENTS

IN THE NOT QUITE DARK

ROGUES

J. J.'s brother, Kenny, was always saying something that J.J. tried not to agree with. A proclamation would come out of Kenny's mouth, and J.J. would say, "That's not true," and then while the word *true* hung there between them, J.J. would realize that he did agree with his brother and hated himself for it. This time Kenny said, "There's too many niggas moving into the neighborhood. It's time to go." J.J. let that idea swirl around in his head, let it touch down and rise again like the funnel cloud of a tornado, and then began to explain, again, why it was uncool for a man of color to complain about too many black people in the neighborhood.

But Kenny just said, "Jay, I ain't got time for your college bullshit right now. Niggas broke into my house and stole my shit!"

They were standing in the middle of Kenny's living room, which had been torn apart by a gang, the Rogues, who had come by on bicycles, Martinez from across the street said.

"They didn't look like anything," he said. "Just boys on bikes ringing the doorbells. But they were Rogues." His arms were crossed so that J.J. could see his purple and faded USMC tattoo.

His green eyes narrowed with vengeance. "Fucking Rogues," he said, and he stroked his shiny goatee, and Kenny lamented the fact that the rottweiler, his security, was dead. "After all that money on health insurance for that dog."

The sun bathed the living room in amber, making all the broken and destroyed glasses, vases, and lamps gleam like pieces of pirate treasure. J.J. stood next to Kenny, across from Martinez, and every time he shifted his foot, he felt and heard the crunch of his sister-in-law's smashed knickknacks. They were swap-meet figurines of black people playing jazz instruments or posed in swing dancing positions or little angels with halos painted unevenly around their curly ceramic hair.

"Why they do this?" Kenny said. "They didn't have to do all this. I wish I *would* catch one of them Negroes tearing up my house."

"This isn't right," Martinez said with certainty.

J.J. was hot, and squeamish about his brother throwing around the n-word. He looked at Martinez, protective of his sensibilities, but he was also looking at Kenny, as if for a game plan.

"It's hot, man," J.J. said. "Turn on the air conditioning?"

His T-shirt was stuck to his back after driving all the way from L.A. in his beat-up Toyota, which, of course, never had air conditioning. He had driven from UCLA, the coolness of a distant ocean breeze turning into dry desert air the deeper he got into the valley and the closer he got to Palm Springs. His brother, his mother and father, had moved miles and miles from Los Angeles, from crime, to homes they could afford. Driving under an overpass, J.J. briefly thought of covered wagons, all the distances people have traveled. But mostly, the landscape reminded him of space, the final frontier. The hills surrounding J.J. as he drove were dry, a combination of pale dirt and jagged rocks, and J.J. always had the feeling that he was driving through some other planet, the Mars or Pluto or Jupiter of *Star Trek* or late-night *Twilight Zone* episodes, land here on

Earth that almost passed as outer space. Driving in his car, his flesh
had cooked for an hour.

Kenny sucked his teeth and rolled up the sleeves of his red
Adidas sweat suit. He was tall, not as tall as J.J., but J.J. always felt
that Kenny loomed over him. Kenny was fifteen years older, and all
his life, J.J. felt as though he had two fathers. Kenny's eyes, barely
visible through his tinted glasses, cut through a person. With those
eyes, people and situations were surveyed, decisions made instantly
and never revisited. Good or bad. Yes or no. Those were the choices
that Kenny gave you. Kenny had just come back from the gym and
had missed the Rogues by about five minutes. The minute Kenny
discovered someone had been in the house, he crossed the street
and got his best friend, Martinez. But J.J. had come in the middle
of the crime scene by accident. He was stopping by to borrow five
hundred bucks from Kenny to make his rent. Kenny hadn't even
known he was coming, but J.J. knew he'd have the money. As he
pulled up, the two men had been crossing the street, slow and easy,
too disgusted and too late to do anything else but have a beer.

Kenny crossed the room, wiping sweat from his shaved head and
taking long strides over his ruined things. Martinez took sips from
his Heineken. Kenny did not seem to hear J.J.'s question about the
air conditioning, so he asked again.

"You want air?" Kenny sipped his beer. "That shit cost money, air
conditioning. Better nigga-rig you a fan or something. There's some
newspaper on the table."

J.J. still didn't know what the deal was about his brother. So
cheap about the weirdest things, things that made a person comfortable, but he thought nothing of blowing his and his wife Joy's
phone-company salary on jewelry or shiny tire rims that spun even
when the car was not in motion, on health insurance for their
dog, who J.J. had resented to the dog's dying day. He had bitten
J.J. when he had tried to feed him, and he shook his head at the

memory. Kenny seemed to think that J.J. was shaking his head about something else. "Sorry, College," Kenny said, winking at Martinez. He pointed his thumb at him and gave Martinez a look. "Scuse my French. *Afro-engineer* that shit. Here." He handed J.J. a newspaper from the table and slapped hands with Martinez. "This makes me want to beat somebody, I swear to God," Kenny said, and he looked around his living room as if it were the first time he'd seen the mess. The brown leather couch had been pulled from the wall for some reason, and the Rogues managed to knock a giant print off the mantel, a portrait of a serene black woman in a white church hat with a wide brim, bowing her head and clutching her white bible. Opposite the portrait, in the hallway, there was a trail of clothes, a jumble of colors and fabrics that spilled into the living room as if someone had been crawling and shedding and suddenly disappeared.

J.J. waved the paper over his face and agreed. It was, in fact, fucked up. But it would have been just as fucked up if white boys had done it. He would have told Kenny this ordinarily. Instead, he said stupidly, "We have a black president now. It's like you're talking about *him* when you're calling people the n-word."

Kenny looked at J.J. with squinting, concerned eyes as though J.J. was suddenly speaking Chinese. He said, "Well Obama don't live in this neighborhood, do he?"

There was a knock on the door while they considered the circumstances. Nobody moved to answer it, and they all watched with suspicion as the door slowly opened. J.J. glanced at his brother for clues. But it was just Kenny's other neighbor, Paul MacNally from two houses over, who let himself in. His flip-flops smacked on the entryway linoleum, and when he saw the mess, he shoved his hands in the pockets of his jeans that were covered in paint.

"Bro. Just got home. Kim told me." He shook his head, and J.J. saw speckles of white paint on his sunburned face, which managed to be both youthful and craggy. "My house. Fucking Martinez's. Now yours. Shit's out of hand, dude." He reached back and tightened his ponytail.

Kenny raised his head, which was bowed down, studying his floor. "Get you a beer, Paul," Kenny said from the couch, and then he pulled his cell phone from the pocket of his sweats. "Calling the cops. They ain't gone do shit, but still."

SUMMERTIME AND J.J. WAS struggling. He worked in the mall, selling cell phones part-time after losing an internship at Intel Finance Group, which he'd gotten through the business school. He had read the internship description and liked the company's favorite activity, "A trip to our Santa Clara headquarters (via our private jets) for finance intern event." He had applied, enticed by the private jets, but failed to "possess a firm grasp of financial statements and their interrelationships." He'd gotten fired, his supervisor said, "for being half-assed and lazy." She had stood behind her large, glass-covered desk then, and walked him to her office door, the smell of her musky perfume trailing behind her. J.J. had reached out to shake her hand and thank her, and she had gripped his hand and pumped it three times meaningfully, her brown, bluntly cut bangs bouncing with each pump, unspoken communication for *Get your shit together*. He double majored in English, the compromise for his parents, who thought going to school for anything that didn't make you money at the end of four years made as much sense as working for free. "I don't care what else you study," his father said, "but the main thing better get you a good job." Now, though, he was qualified to do exactly nothing that would get him through his last summer before senior year. He had never been a waiter, bartender, retailer, host, mechanic, accountant, bus driver. Two years at Taco Bell summed up his experience before college, and during the school year he was a work-study student stuffing envelopes and running errands for the campus news service. And English? What was he thinking? English was like a pretty girl you had a crush on. Just because you thought you loved her, it didn't mean you had to have her. And yet he couldn't stop thinking about how much he wanted her. All the places they went together when he was a boy, while his parents fought over money. *What happened to that twenty dollars? Why you buy name brand? Why you shop at Ralphs? You should have went to Stater Brothers. Ralphs groceries too high!* J.J. just kept turning pages, traveling distances far, far away from home. But now, where to go? How to get there? How to make a living? There was the Peace Corps. He could volunteer. Some place in Africa? But when he thought about doing something noble like that, he could only think about being broke. He was only twenty-one, but he already felt like he wanted to start over. "And all this time you could have been making money," Kenny always said. "Could have got you on at the phone company. Benefits and everything. I swear you don't have sense."

What he had been hoping for at Kenny's was a pop-in, grab-the-money, pop-out type of deal, but instead he was in the middle of a mess that was going to take a while. Kenny had a plan. It was early evening now, and everybody sat in the dining room while the television played on the kitchen counter and the lights from the pool shimmered in the backyard, just over Martinez's shoulder. Beyond the backyard fence, the mountains looked close enough to touch, dark shadows layered in blues, purples, and reds. The mess in the living room was cleaned up, and the figurines that were left looked lonely to J.J. Every time he glanced at them, they looked back at him with shiny, off-centered pupils as if to say, *Do something!*

"This is what we need to do," Kenny said. He played with the jumble of diamonds that ringed his pinky. The only ring he had left, since the Rogues took most of his other jewelry. Insured or not, his stuff was still gone, and he was pissed. "We have to watch out. Everybody really pay attention the next few days. Starting tonight. I mean stay up late if you have to. Police came and took their little fingerprints and whatnot, but I ain't holding my breath for some kind of Columbo shit to happen where they gone magically find these niggas with my valuables gift-wrapped with *To Kenny* on a tag or some bullshit."

J.J.'s sister-in-law, Joy, sat next to Kenny and sipped her wine. She still had on her makeup from her workday at the phone company but was wearing pink terry cloth sweats with a matching hoodie. She had divided her long dreadlocks into two ponytails, and to J.J. she looked like she could be one of their children. "Stop saying *nigger*, Kenny," she said tonelessly, sounding bored with her own request.

Kenny ate a handful of popcorn and washed it down with a sip of beer. "I pay a twelve-hundred-dollar house note every month and I'm sitting in my house, at my table, eating food I bought, so nigga, nigga, nigga."

"You're crazy, dude," Paul said with a smile, a careful smile, J.J. thought. Paul's eyes crinkled in the corners, and he had creases there even when he wasn't smiling, but his mouth was a straight line of politeness.

Martinez said, "Well." He had switched over to water. "I gotta work in, like, eight hours, but I could watch after."

"Not me, dude," Paul said. "My two jobs are killing me. Paint in the day and my graveyard shift at the plant, bro."

Kenny looked at Joy, and when she leveled her eyes at him, he looked away. "Right." She rose from the table and yawned. "Don't get your asses kicked by little kids," she said, and she disappeared around the kitchen corner.

"Well." Kenny pushed his beer can around the circles. "I have to get some sleep tonight because I have to pull a double tomorrow."

Everybody nodded with understanding, and Kenny gave J.J. a hard look. He shrugged and held his hands up. What?

"I mean, it's not like you got shit to do," Kenny said, and J.J. thought that if he was going to borrow money, *again*, that the least he could do would be to keep watch, at least for one night. But after, he would ask about the money. Now, he was a volunteer out of the goodness of his heart.

THEY STOOD IN THE garage, whispering. It was twelve thirty in the morning, and Kenny explained the mission. J.J. was going to sit in a lawn chair between the closed garage door and Kenny's enormous black Hummer that J.J. had told him not to lease because it was bad for the environment—and tacky. He tried again. "This car. Conspicuous, bro," J.J. said. "Conspicuous consumption. Plain and simple."

"As hard as I work?" Kenny said. "I will buy, lease, or drive whatever the fuck kind of car I want to. You can drive that busted-up Toyota, *professor*," he said, and he stroked the back of the car. He left a clean streak through the fine dust. "People see me coming when I drive this car."

It had to be ninety degrees in the darkness. The breeze blew the palm trees that lined the streets, and the streetlights were on, but J.J. would still be hidden when he sat down in the chair. In the distance, he could see the silhouette of the hills that had a big white *M* for Moreno Valley. Somebody close by was playing something being sung in Spanish, and a dog in a nearby yard barked rhythmically, three yelps at a time. "You good?" Kenny put his hand on his brother's shoulder. He yawned. J.J. yawned too, watching his brother. He wanted to be able to listen to the oldies station, to read his book of E. E. Cummings poems, but it was too dark to read, and any kind of noise would give him away.

"Yeah, I'm good."

"First thing you see or hear that's shady, you come and get me. Wake my ass up, all right?"

J.J. nodded.

"For real."

"Yeah," J.J. said. "For reals. I will."

"Check it out." Kenny pointed. "See that light way over there?" Kenny followed his brother's finger and saw a soft, solitary light twinkling in the distance. "Somebody just built that house. It's *nice*. I drove up to it the other day, but they got a big-ass fence around it." Kenny jutted his chin out toward a house across the street. "It ain't like over there." New people had moved in and left a couch on the sidewalk in front of their house. They had three beat-up cars, and one of them, a lime green Plymouth Fury, was up on blocks. "Look at that." He rolled up his sleeves as though he was getting ready for something other than bed. "What did I tell you about this neighborhood?"

ONE HOUR WENT BY. It was one thirty. Cars went down the street, and then fewer did. It was two. Two thirty. The street got quiet, and nothing happened. A young girl and boy walked by, with a stroller. The boy wore a dark hoodie, which made J.J. sit up straight, suspicious. But they walked by without saying anything or doing anything. Two young people taking a walk with their baby. That was all. Nothing, nothing, and J.J. was falling asleep when he heard a car driving by slowly. He was suddenly alert, one eye peering around the edge of the Hummer. A tan Toyota stopped in the middle of the street, directly in front of the house opposite Kenny's. He saw two figures gesturing and nodding. One looked bigger than the other; the other could very well be a child. What to do? What should he do? He got up from his chair and walked alongside the Hummer to the hatchback of the car and pretended to fiddle with it. "Damn," he said, loud enough to be heard, and he pulled on the door. "I forgot my key." He turned around to face the two figures in the idling car behind him. "Hey," J.J. said, his hands shaking, and they drove off without answering.

"AIN'T NOBODY TOLD YOU to conversate with them motherfuckers," Kenny said the next morning after J.J. reported what had happened. He was gesticulating with his coffee, and some of it splashed on the counter. The house was warm already, even though it was only seven in the morning. The sun was casting a golden hue on the hills beyond the backyard. On the television, there were some good-natured barbs traded between the morning-show hosts.

"I just said 'hey,'" J.J. said.

Kenny worked his jaw. "Hey," Kenny mimicked in a high voice that was supposed to be J.J.'s. "Hey, I've lost my damn mind." He put his coffee cup down so he could use both hands to make his point. "Where my mind at?" he asked, sounding like a girl. "Jay. Those fools might have a gun. *My* gun that they stole. Do not talk to them. Just watch. Watch what they do. Stay out the way. I swear you don't have sense. Can you get a degree in Sense?"

J.J. watched Kenny drink his coffee, as if he were mad at it. While Kenny stood in the kitchen, J.J. tried to bring himself to ask him for money. It was morning, and it was just the two of them. No Joy, no Martinez or Paul. Still, he couldn't bring himself to do it. He had no sense. How could a person who had no sense ask for money? He watched Kenny walk out the door to his job at the phone company, making guaranteed money. On the dining room wall were two mortarboards of Kenny and Joy's boys, who had graduated from high school already. They were a year apart, J.J.'s nephews, and now they were in the military. Kenny and Joy had

had them early. Kenny had been seventeen and Joy had been six-teen, and now J.J. felt like their third child, struggling with money, trying to get through school. J.J. and Kenny's parents weren't the ones to go to if you needed money. They believed in every man for himself. Hold onto the boot, and don't break the strap. But that's what he got for being the smart one, Kenny always said. He'd thought of high school and college as something that got in the way of him making a living. "I'd rather be the dumb motherfucker with money any day." But J.J. was always telling Kenny that money was overrated. Hummers and jewelry, well, J.J. was always saying that he didn't want any part of it.

MARTINEZ HAD THE DAY shift, and so J.J. left it to him. Joy was at work too, and since Martinez was on the lookout for the Rogues, J.J. didn't have all that much to do. The water called out to him—it had to be a hundred degrees—and so he started out in the Jacuzzi and then moved over to the pool. He kept his blended margaritas on hand and helped himself to the mixed nuts in the pantry. If he had a thousand bucks, he could get to the end of summer, another month, with his part-time cell phone money. He was only going to ask for five hundred now, and then ask for the other five hundred later. That's how he had to do it, get the money in little pieces, little installments, so that Kenny wouldn't really think of it like he was just handing over a thousand bucks all of a sudden. It made him feel bad, as if he were sneaking off with his brother's money when he wasn't looking, but Kenny had it to burn. And if he had so much, what was wrong with getting a little of it? With more money, J.J. could relax a little bit, slow down and take some time in figuring out what he was going to do. Was he going to get a job that made him some money? Or do some-thing else, like go back to school to keep studying? Maybe he'd buy a few books even, with his five-hundred-dollar windfall. J.J. dreamed of this, of bookshelves lined with books. Kenny dreamed of Hummers and diamond pinky rings. Both dreams were the dreams of their parents, now retired, who lived on fixed incomes. They wanted their sons to be educated, and they wanted their sons to have enough money. J.J. and Kenny split the difference. They split on a lot of things, split their votes in the Democratic primaries, even. "How can you not vote Obama, man?" J.J. had demanded over tequila shots that Kenny had been steadily supplying as they drank in the bar in the Chili's around the corner from Kenny's house.

"Money pure and simple," Kenny had hollered over the three TVs blaring in the bar. "You got a lot to learn, little bro. Hillary will take care of the money. Fuck a Barack Obama."

J.J. submerged his head and let the sun brown him. It was going on two o'clock, and he thought he should be doing something. He got out of the pool and lay in a lounge chair. He decided to call his ex-girlfriend, Jennifer, who he had broken up with because she started talking about the kids they would have. The apartment they would live in. She had this idea for their lives: her nursing degree, J.J.'s healthy salary after his business degree, little league and church and barbecues with their neighbors, movie night, bowling night. When she talked like this, J.J. felt his throat tighten, like two enormous invisible hands were strangling him. But now he was missing her, thinking of the boy and the girl walking their baby on his stakeout last night. He called, after two months of them ignoring each other. Her voice mail answered, and her sing-song-y voice conjured up her image, her smooth brown skin with red undertones, her heart-shaped lips that always tasted like watermelon lip gloss. The long braids down her back. *Hi, this is Jennifer, holla at me!* But J.J. held the phone to his ear at the beep. Then he hung up.

Three margaritas and two hours later, he was still in the pool. A bumblebee touched down on the surface of the water, took a drink, and buzzed off. "Hey, bee. Hey, man. What's the story? Where you going, bee?" J.J. asked. It was then that J.J. realized he'd gotten himself drunk, and he decided to get out of the pool. He dried himself off and wandered across the street to Martinez's, taking his margarita with him. Martinez sat in his garage, in his lawn chair, listening to the Dodgers. When he saw J.J. coming, he got up and unfolded a chair for him.

"No news?" J.J. sipped his margarita and let his eyes glide over a picture of Muhammad Ali hanging on the wall. Boxes hung on shelves, and a fake Christmas tree branch poked out of the top, touching the ceiling as though feeling its way out. He saw a dart-board and thought about asking Martinez for a game.

"You look dark, man," Martinez said. "You been tanning or something?"

J.J. almost told him that black folks didn't lie out trying to get dark. They just got dark without trying.

"No news?" he said again.

"Dodgers are messing up, man. They can't play worth shit." Martinez twisted his lips in disgust. "How they gonna give up three hits and a home run and the inning ain't even close to being over?"

J.J. nodded. "No news about the Rogues, though?"

Martinez pulled on his T-shirt and blew through the opening of the neck. "Fucking *hot*. And I haven't seen Rogue *one*."

J.J. shook his head sadly and sat with Martinez until the Dodgers lost the game. Soon after, Joy came home and waved from across the street, and then Kenny, pulling up in his Hummer, 50 Cent blaring. He crossed the street, and when he got closer, he frowned.

"Goddamn, nigga, what happened to *you*? Looking like a *African*. Like a Negro just rubbed *Crisco* all over himself and *dared* the sun."

"He looks dark, right?" Martinez said.

"Don't call me that, Kenny," J.J. said, suddenly exhausted.

"I'm just saying," Kenny said. He rubbed his hand over his shaved head. "You ain't seen anybody?"

"Nah," Martinez said. "It's been dead."

"I'm on it tonight," Kenny said. "I'm a catch these fools. You watch." He turned to J.J. "You still in?" J.J. thought of his five hundred dollars he had yet to ask for. "Yeah, I'm in."

THEY SET UP THREE chairs behind the Hummer and lined up at one in the morning. Kenny was on one end, Paul was in the middle, and J.J. sat on the other end. It took them a while to settle in. Kenny told J.J. to put that shit away when he tried to text out of boredom. "See how bright that light is? Might as well call out to them motherfuckers and tell them we're sitting here. They can probably see that crazy Afro of yours, too. This is how you supposed to look," he said, rubbing his own smooth head. "Keep it down, dude," Paul said. "They're going to hear us if you keep talking shit." And J.J. couldn't stand the smell of Kenny's cigar smoke wafting in his face. "Man, seriously," J.J. said the second time Kenny accidentally or on purpose blew smoke in his direction. "What am I doing in the middle?" Paul said after a while. The night breeze passed over them, and Paul tipped his head back and smiled. He looked like he was getting his temples massaged by an invisible masseuse. He took off his flip-flops so that he was barefoot and then abruptly snapped his head forward. "I can't see anything," he said. "I'm just staring at the back of the Hummer."

After a while, no one had any more observations or complaints. They sat there in the moonlight, passing tic-tac-toe back and forth, the occasional hangman. A man got hanged when J.J. chose the word *Spumante*. When all the letters got filled in, Paul and Kenny silently studied the page and then looked at each other.

Paul motioned for the pen and wrote something down, then passed the paper to Kenny, who silently convulsed, holding his fist to his mouth. He passed the paper to J.J., and it read "spu-stupid." J.J. was tired of hangman anyway. He shut his eyes one moment, and the next moment, Kenny was shaking his shoulders and pointing. Kenny held his fingers to his lips. Shhhh. Paul and Kenny slowly stood, and J.J. watched their heads turn as their eyes followed their target. When J.J. stood, all he saw was what looked like a little boy carrying a pillowcase. "Hey!" Kenny said, and he ran toward the kid, who started running too. J.J. looked at Paul, who shrugged and took off after Kenny. By the time J.J. had decided that he was going to run after them, they had already caught the boy, and so J.J. jogged toward the scene. Kenny had the kid by one hand, and Paul had him by the other. J.J. stared at the boy, who didn't look any older than eleven or twelve years old. He was light-skinned with neat, cornrowed hair and was wearing beat-up brown Converse.

"Remind me never to need your ass," Kenny said, breathing hard. "Paul's barefoot and he got here faster than you."

"This is just a kid," J.J. said. "This can't be one of the Rogues. You need to let him go."

"Get off me," the kid said. He broke away from Paul and tried to twist out of Kenny's grip. J.J. looked around, nervous. Was this some kind of abuse? This was somebody's child. The streetlights shone a fuzzy yellow light down on all of them, and when J.J. looked, up, he was disgusted at the sight of all the gnats and mosquitoes swarming up against each other, fighting for the light.

"Kenny, man, Paul. Seriously," J.J. said. "Hold up." He was much taller than the boy, and so he bent down so that his face was level with his. "What are you doing out here, man? It's like two in the morning."

"That's what I'm saying," Kenny said. He jerked the kid on the last word. "And what's in that bag? Other people's shit that you done already stole?"

"Man," the kid said. He scrunched up his face. "Who you supposed to be?"

Paul snatched the pillowcase and walked over to the streetlight so that he could see inside better. He pulled out a pair of shiny black dress shoes.

"Nice," he said. He held them up like he was offering them to Kenny and J.J. "These are nice."

Kenny stared the boy down. "What you doing with those shoes?"

"My dad's, man." And then the boy told a story about living up the street but then his father couldn't pick him up even though it was late and that's why he was walking late at night. "Dang. Can't I walk down the street?"

"What about those shoes, though," Kenny said. "Where they come from?"

"My friend's dad is giving them to my dad." He looked at all three men. "He needs them. We just moved in, and we don't have a lot of money."

Paul looked down at his bare feet and then looked out the corner of his eyes at Kenny. Kenny let go of the kid finally. "Look. There's been some bullshit happening in the neighborhood. You look like you might be one of the kids that's running around here stealing shit. You know anything about that?"

The boy shook his head. "Why I look like one of those dudes to you? What those other dudes look like?"

Exactly, J.J thought, and he watched his brother's eyes as he decided not to answer the boy's question the way he would have answered had J.J. asked him.

"Too bad Martinez is at work right now," J.J. said. "We could let him take a look at this kid so you'd be satisfied." He gave his brother a told-you-so look.

"Sorry, little man," Kenny said. "We straight. Better get home."

The boy walked over to Paul and yanked the pillowcase out of his hands. "Sorry, dude," Paul said. "What's your name, anyway?"

The boy backed away from the three of them, and his face became less defined the farther away he got. Then he took off running. "My name is fuck you!" he screamed in the darkness, and two or three lights came on in the neighborhood, but nobody came outside.

J.J. WAS ON THE couch watching *Oprah* for the third day in a row. He had just gotten out of the pool and sat barefoot with no shirt on, drinking a beer. He had ended up staying in Moreno Valley for days. "I'm sick," he told his boss when he called in, using his best phlegmy cough. He still hadn't asked Kenny for money, and so he used the stakeouts as an excuse for his extended stay. After the boy, though, the stakeouts were half-assed. They did one the very next night, but Paul, Martinez, and J.J. got to talking, and then someone turned on the radio and J.J. suggested a game of pool. After so many beers it was two thirty in the morning and nothing going on in the neighborhood anyway. J.J. spent the rest of the week reading and lounging in the pool until Kenny asked him, "When are you leaving? Or pay me some rent, eating all my goddamn food, J.J."

Yesterday's *Oprah* was a repeat of Oprah's Favorite Things, and J.J. had started out the hour smugly mocking all the women falling apart over all the free-but-expensive items they were getting. And that episode where she gave everybody a *car*, J.J. remembered. It would have been cool to be just *given* a car. Today, the women on television were so grateful to be made over, and J.J. judged them for their gratitude. Clothes, they were just clothes, ladies. No need for tears. But then he wondered: Was this his problem? If it worked for these women, maybe it would work for him. Maybe he simply needed to be made over. In the middle of the television tears, J.J.

heard shouts from outside. He heard his name being called. "Jay! Yo, Jay!" It was Martinez. J.J. ran into the street. "What? What's going on?"

Martinez wiped his face with his Def Leppard T-shirt. "They hit the Pedregons' house, man. They're not home, but I saw three little dudes running out of the house, and it wasn't no Pedregons."

"Call the cops, then!" J.J. squinted from the sun and rubbed his hands together because he didn't know what else to do. He looked like a television villain, crafty and scheming. "Call the cops!"

"I did already!" Martinez yelled. "I did already. In broad daylight," Martinez said, shaking his head. "These fucking kids are crazy."

While they waited for the cops, J.J. happened to look over at his Toyota that had been parked and ignored for days. Now he was looking at shattered glass on the pavement and peering into the car, which now had no radio. How much was that going to cost? The window and the radio? "My car! Martinez, did you see this shit?" He was already in the hole, and now he was going to have to replace his window. Try to replace his radio. He felt like crying.

Two cops eventually arrived in their squad car. When they arrived, J.J. was sitting on the curb, picking pieces of glass out of his feet. Martinez was standing over him with his hands folded, watching. One other neighbor, Mr. Stone, leaned on his cane and directed J.J. on how to get out the more elusive pieces of glass. Wisps of his thin gray hair blew up over his head like swirling white cotton candy, and he kept pushing his glasses up his sweaty nose. J.J. briefly thought about what he must have looked like. Skin ashy from the pool. No shirt, no shoes. Bloody feet. One cop regarded him. He was dark-skinned and enormous, hours spent in the gym, no doubt. His partner was lanky, with red hair fashioned into a crew cut. Officer Odell, his tag read. He said, "Is this the suspect?" He pointed at J.J.

"What?" J.J. stood up, and the officers took a few steps back. "Do I look like I just robbed somebody?"

"Well, yeah," the black officer said. Officer Keane. "You kind of do."

J.J. patted his Afro and pulled up his shorts. Then he sat back down on the curb and put his face in his hands.

The officers shrugged and exchanged glances. They looked at Martinez and Mr. Stone for guidance. Mr. Stone said, "He got glass in his feet." Martinez said, "No, no, no. These kids were little, an older one too," and J.J. knew exactly what one of the kids looked like. *That little . . .*

A little girl happened by on her bicycle. She slowed down and made two tight circles before she stopped. She stood, her legs wide on either side of her pink bike, her multiple braids held together by dozens of tiny barrettes stuck in her hair like confetti. The white stick of a sucker jutted out of her mouth, and she tilted her head, staring at J.J., a curiosity.

Officer Odell looked at J.J. "What? What did you say? He was little?"

"I know what one of them looked like, at least," J.J. said.

"Well, what then?" Officer Odell said. Beads of sweat were forming on his face, and his black uniform looked heavy and hot.

J.J. hesitated. He couldn't be sure of what to say about these boys and how to say it. He wanted to be right, do right. But they could be described in many ways, these boys who took from people, who had nothing and wanted something for nothing. J.J. knew what Kenny would say, how he would describe them and leave the thought of them behind. But how would he describe his own brother, sitting on a curb, surrounded by two police officers? He contemplated the jagged rocks on the hills looking like some other planet. There was that lonely house in the distance, just under the sun, the home of somebody who had built something just a little bit beyond the rest of the people.

"Hey," Officer Keane said. "I'm talking to you. Stand up. You need to stand up while I'm talking to you in the first place." J.J. stood, dusting off the back of his shorts. The house looked close enough, but it wasn't. It was far away. J.J. wondered: What kind of people were those, living in that house? Martinez and Mr. Stone stared at him, waiting. The little girl crunched on her sucker. Officer Keane shifted his weight. "Well?" He cleared his throat. He was tired of waiting on J.J. He said, "Answer the question, young man."

SUNSHINE

For their anniversaries, other women get, what? Like a box of chocolate and roses if they got a boring boyfriend, or dinner at the Olive Garden or someplace like that if the guy's half-trying. A stuffed animal? Or even jewelry, if he's for real. Not no cheap bastard. *Something*. Me, I get something else not even close. I get Bobby coming home from work a few weeks before, telling me somebody there at the gym has a crush on me. He was all excited, grinning like he had new teeth and wanted to show them off.

I didn't get what he was up to. Not because I wasn't hella smart. I was. Bobby admitted that one time after we did it for an hour in the desert, in Palmdale somewhere, in the middle of nowhere. I'd taken this astronomy class at L.A. City College because I had a lot of time on my hands, and I was learning a lot about stars and stuff. I told Bobby about how all the stars were just distant suns and that the sun we saw in the daytime was just the largest of all the suns; of all a hundred billion suns—at least. The largest object in our whole big crazy solar system. He squeezed me really hard. "Damn, you're smart," he said. Bobby waited till I gave him a big sunshine smile, and then he said, "But everybody ain't perfect."

Ha, I'd said.

But lately I was hardly smart enough to know what he was up to anymore, because since his brother had died, Bobby treated everything like a big hurry. He didn't take time for anything—or when he did, it was like he forgot why he was taking the time in the first place. He was treating his life like something he wanted to get over with, to do, but not to see.

He was still grinning at me about this crush, so I asked him, "What? You glad some man at your work's wanting me? That don't sound like you, Bobby." What sounded like Bobby was jealousy. He made me quit stripping because of it. I put my hand on his forehead, and he slapped it back down.

"Quit playing with the smart-ass comments." He ran his hand through his wavy black hair and stared at me. He was dyeing it because he was only thirty-six and going gray.

I stared back. "So? Who's this guy?" All this time Bobby was standing in front of me in his favorite gray sweat suit. He unzipped his jacket, tossed it on the futon, and started making his way to the kitchen to cook.

"You thaw that chicken like I told you?"

"It's in the sink. Is it that Furio guy? That actor guy?" He worked out at the gym, and he was always giving me the eye.

"Please," Bobby said. "Where the fuck's the olives? I was going to make cacciatore."

"Ate em."

"Okay, Big Ass," Bobby said. "That's the last thing you should be eating. A whole goddamn *can*?" He shook his head. "I'm just going to broil this, then. What else you eat up in here?"

Bobby Cantadopolous was militant about cooking, his kitchen, food, and me involved with any of these things. I'd moved in with him in his apartment, and it always felt that way—like his.

"Who's got the crush on me, Bobby? I'm tired of waiting for you to tell me." I just knew it was some nasty dude. Otherwise, Bobby wouldn't think it was so damn funny. "What's his name?"

Bobby was washing the chicken and was seasoning it. He looked up at me, mouth serious, eyes cracking up. "Amber."

"Amber? Amber," I repeated. Bobby got me to thinking. "Is it that transsexual dude? The one who just came back with all the changes?"

"Uh-uh," Bobby said.

"Amber," I said again. I watched Bobby chop onion and crush garlic. "Is this dude, like, Irish or something? Got one of them names that sounds like a lady? Like Carol or Adrian? Like that?"

"Nope," Bobby said. "And whoever heard of a guy named Amber?"

Bobby poured olive oil in the pan and stirred in the onion and garlic. I was hungry. "We eating rice with that?"

"No, *we* ain't," Bobby said. He was policing my weight more since I quit stripping. I wasn't doing a lot of exercising no more. "Broccoli for you, rice for me."

"Fuck," I said.

"Watch it, tough guy. Keep that filth out your mouth."

I rolled my eyes. "So *who*, Bobby? I practically don't give a shit anymore."

He gave me the eyebrows and then swatted me on the ass. "What I tell you?"

I leaned against the counter with my arms crossed, pouting. Bobby tap-danced on my nerves sometimes. He concentrated on browning the chicken, stirring it around and staring at it like it was his life's work. Finally, he said, "Remember that thing I did down in Mexico last year? With the four girls?"

"Yeah," I said slow. That was before me and Bobby were together, when he was just starting to do porn. It don't matter to me, the porn on the side of training folks at the gym. I'm just saying, Mexico was a long time ago, at least a year. Telling me about it when we first met, Bobby bragged that he made eight hundred dollars just to go down to Mexico and be with a bunch of women. I thought eight hundred dollars was a bit cheap to have your life out there, floating around forever and ever, but he said he would've been with all those women for free.

"I guess," I'd said, and Bobby'd said that was the trouble with me. I never opened my eyes to see the bigger picture.

But now I was trying. "What's Mexico got to do with all that?" Before Bobby could answer, I got a picture in my head of this blond woman he was always talking about like something he missed, like his mother's home-baked cookies, waiting for him after school on a rainy day. "*Amber*," I said. I sucked my teeth and rolled my eyes at Bobby. She had blown him in this other video he did.

"Yeah, right? The blond? With the tiny waist and the lips?" He tore his eyes away from the chicken long enough to bite down hard on his fist. "Fuckin A," he said.

"If you want to call those lips," I said. "They look like life rafts. A little collagen goes a long way. You should tell her that."

"You're one to talk," Bobby said. He motioned a finger and then tapped his lips, so I could come to him and kiss him.

I stood where I was. "On me, it looks normal. You ever see a black girl with thin lips? No. You ain't," I said.

"Eh, what're ya gonna do," he said and shrugged, like some things you just can't help. He finally stopped babying his chicken, mixed everything together, and put it in the broiler. When he straightened up, he stretched out his arms and wiggled his fingers. "What I tell you? Get over here and give me a kiss."

I was getting worked up. "No, and what's so great about her ass?"

"Nice and big."

"But you keep telling me that mine's getting *too* big. What's up with that?"

"Since when did *big* mean *gigantic*? Huh? Answer me that, Whole-Can-a-Olives."

Because I was hugging myself and wouldn't come to him, Bobby came to me and put his arms around my waist. "I'm just breaking your balls, you know that, right?" He kissed me and held me so close and tight that I felt wrapped up, completely. His hands traveled down my waist and under my ass. "I'm just giving you a hard time. I might even let you eat some rice—if you go to the gym tomorrow. Get on that treadmill."

I laughed, waiting for Bobby to say, "Just kidding." But he didn't.

Late in the night, when I was trying to fall asleep, Bobby wouldn't shut up about Amber. What if she hit on me, would I do her? Didn't I think she was sorta cute? Would I do it, just for him even? Just for fun? What was the big deal? It wasn't like he was asking me to be with another man. What'd I think?

I told him that I thought he was a sex fiend, but if he was nice to me, I just might. And he finally shut up, which was all I wanted. In bed with Bobby, when it was quiet, was the only time I could talk to him about serious things. So I asked him how his mother was doing with Louie being gone. It had only been three months.

"How you think she's doing?" he said, and then I didn't hear anything else from him. We just lay there in the dark.

Before long he was snoring, holding on to me tight, his left arm lying across my body like a weight. This threesome thing seemed to come out of nowhere, but Bobby did seem restless, a little wilder since his brother died. Bobby says I'm full of shit when I say he changed after his brother got killed. But how could he not? Louie was his heart, a younger version of Bobby, a nice kid with a big mouth. Louie took to calling me Sunshine, just like Bobby. Some asshole shot him at the ATM and only got forty bucks off him. I was there when Bobby got the phone call from his father. Bobby'd just gotten off me. We were happy, wiped out. When the phone rang, he got up, went to the phone, and stood there naked. We had two candles burning, and the moon was so bright that we didn't even need them. And Bobby, Bobby was so beautiful to me, the curves of his muscles, hard and rocky with smooth, shiny skin from the sweat on his body. I don't remember what Bobby said, if he said anything into the phone. He just fell to his knees and dropped the phone. His daddy was hollering, "Bobby! Bobby!" in a tiny cartoon voice, coming from the phone, but Bobby was curled up in a ball with his eyes squeezed shut and his mouth wide open. Nothing coming out. When I went to him, Bobby grabbed me and held on to me so hard that I thought he was going to crush something inside me. I knew his kid brother was dead. Nobody had to tell me nothing.

When I tried to get out of going to the funeral with Bobby— because his family was always asking if he was still dating me, the black *kariola*, and did he think he was the fucking Greek Robert De Niro, with the black chicks every time they turned around— Bobby told me, "La Donna, fuck them. I need you there." I asked him what *kariola* meant, and he told me, "Never mind. It ain't nice." At the funeral, Bobby held my hand tight and leaned forward in his chair while they dropped dirt onto the casket. Then they lowered the casket into the grave. Bobby didn't really cry until then, and later he told me it was because his brother was deep in the dirt, covered with dirt, and was going to turn into dirt. I told Bobby that Louie wasn't in the casket. Louie's *body* was there, covered in dirt, but the Louie that Bobby loved—his spirit—was with us and the whole world. Bobby told me to shut up and kissed me on the forehead, so I knew I made him feel better, some kind of way.

"That's why I love you, Donna," he said. He took my hand. "You know how to take care of me, Sunshine."

Now, Bobby was snoring even louder, his mouth open just a little bit. I turned my head to kiss him on the lips. They felt soft, and I wanted him to wake up and make love to me. I kissed him again and played with the black waves of his hair. But he didn't feel a thing. He just kept right on sleeping.

BOBBY WORKED OUT AND trained at Gold's Gym off Santa Monica Boulevard. Sometimes famous people worked out there. Like I care. One time, though? Bobby almost broke his neck in three places trying to get a look at some skinny model bitch, and that pissed me off. Kind of wished he'd broken *something*.

Getting to the gym was the same routine every time. It took us a thousand stoplights to get down Santa Monica, park the car, give the homeless guy in the parking lot a couple of bucks for wiping down Bobby's Mustang, Bobby "how ya doin" everybody, me wishing I was at Zankou Chicken eating a drumstick. When we walked in, Bobby gave me the regimen.

"Cardio . . . You gotta hit the ab machine, no doubt. And after that, some lunges." He raised his voice over the techno crap they were playing, and he looked around the gym, scanning the joint like he was looking for someone.

"This really, really sucks," I said.

"What?" Bobby wasn't paying attention. He was looking around the gym.

"If you hadn't made me quit dancing, I would still be lean." I made sure I said it right in his ear so he could hear me over the bass and noise from all the clinking weights and machines.

"Lean," Bobby said. "You a lot of things, baby, but better cross *lean* off the list." He laughed. He was cracking himself up. "I got a appointment," he said. "See you about an hour."

When Bobby walked away, I couldn't help but notice that he *did* look good in his wife-beater tank top against his tan skin. From the tanning salon, but still. That's why I put up with him, I thought. That, and he always looked out for me, was always on my side. I told myself that he had me at the gym for my health, for my own good. Plus, once—and only once—he told me that I was so fine, he didn't need to do nothing to make himself look good. I did it for him.

I found a StairMaster and stepped on it, bored off my ass after two steps. I pushed the button that made the machine go faster— but not too fast. I daydreamed I was at the club I used to dance at, the Eight Ball, where I met Bobby. Those were good days. I missed the girls, and I missed the money. I worked where I wanted to work, doing what I wanted to do. I didn't have to do any of that gym shit.

Somebody was talking to me. Amber.

"It's better if you lower the resistance. If you're just wanting definition. You don't want to cover your body with a lot of muscle," she said in a soft, clear voice. She sounded like a therapist.

"Yeah," I said. I gave her a half-smile. A polite, now-you-can-go smile. She didn't seem to catch what I was doing, though. She stretched some, and then she got on the StairMaster next to mine. She was wearing one of those I'm-at-the-gym-to-be-looked-at out-fits. Cute and strappy. Whenever I tried to wear something like that, Bobby told me to put some clothes on. She worked out on the machine next to me, taking cute little baby steps and swinging her white-blond ponytail around. Everything about her was slight and golden tanned. If somebody was looking for the opposite of me, they would have pointed out Amber in a heartbeat. What was the matter with Bobby?

The whole time I was working out, she kept looking at me out of the corner of her eye, making me nervous. I never knew no woman who had a crush on me before. I didn't know how I felt about it. I ignored Amber until Bobby came up behind me and told me to stop leaning. That was cheating, he said. It wasn't good to cheat. Made the whole workout easier.

"Just pretend you're on the stairway to heaven, baby," he said. "And I'm up there waiting for you." I swear, Bobby thought he was a regular actor, a porn actor, a trainer, *and* a comedian.

"La Donna can cheat," Amber said. My name sounded funny coming out of her mouth. She stopped stepping and looked me up and down. "She doesn't even need to work out."

"Riiiiiight," Bobby said slowly. "Uh-huh."

"La Donna has the most beautiful body in the world. And face, too," Amber said. She winked at me.

"Tiny fuckin world, eh?" Bobby said. "Yeah? Right?" He looked at Amber for a laugh, but she didn't give it to him. "I'm just kiddin, baby," he said. He popped me on the ass.

"Then why'd you say it?" Amber asked him.

"C'mon," Bobby said. "Donna knows I'm joking, right, baby?"

I gave Bobby my fuck-you eyes. I was kind of pissed at both of them for talking like I wasn't there.

"Anyway, it's not a tiny world. It's a big, big world, Bobby," Amber said. She stared at me. "A whole universe."

Bobby looked at Amber and then at me. "You want we should get some lunch? Maybe I could make us something at the house. I got a bottle of wine, too." He put on the sweet-and-innocent face. I got loose with wine, Bobby knew. He looked back and forth at me and Amber.

"I've got a previous engagement," Amber said. "Engagement" sounded like she'd added "loser" to the end of it. Bobby just hadn't paid attention. "But, La Donna?" She pulled the band from her ponytail and shook her hair out. "Maybe if we're around here together sometime, we could have a coffee or something."

"That sounds good," Bobby said. But Amber ignored him and touched my hand. "Nice talking to you," she said.

"Be good," Bobby said, and then she gave him the smile I'd given to her earlier. Now go away.

•

THERE WAS GOING TO be what they called an annular eclipse, my astronomy teacher said. On Bobby's and my anniversary, this was going to happen. Professor Salazar spent a whole class period talking about how annular eclipses come once every couple of years or so and only happen when the moon passes right in front of the sun. But it's not able to cover the sun the whole way, because the moon looks smaller than the sun. I thought that was all pretty cool. Stuff I hadn't really thought about. I was trying to tell Bobby all this when we were sitting in front of the TV, watching some dating show where one person goes on a date with a bunch of people and has to get rid of them one by one until they end up with the person they really want.

"And you know what else, Bobby? I learned something else. The moon?" I looked over at him to make sure he was still listening. He didn't seem to be, but I kept talking anyway. "The moon? It's this, like, cold rocky ball of stuff. Doesn't have its own light coming from it. You know why the moon looks so bright at night, Bobby?"

"Why?" He pulled me to him and starting twirling one of my braids in his fingers. "Can you believe this? This moron's gonna pick the short girl, the one with the mouth on her, always talking all the time. They oughtta let me on the show." He blew out some air, disgusted.

I snuggled up against Bobby and rubbed his belly under his T-shirt.

"That's nice," he said. "Keep doing that."

"I was telling you about the moon," I whispered, and I kissed him on the soft part underneath his armpit. Bobby got still when I did that.

"What about it?" His voice was soft and low, way down his throat.

"I learned that the reason the moon looks so bright is because of the sun. We wouldn't even see the moon if it wasn't for the sun."

"Fascinatin," Bobby said. He undid the top button of his jeans and waited for me to do the rest.

AMBER ALWAYS SEEMED TO find me at the gym. This time, I was just finishing my workout when she came up to me. I was sweating so much, I looked like I'd just gotten hosed down. I walked real slow on the treadmill and slowed down the speed until I was barely walking. When Amber walked up to me, she said, "I hate the tread-mill. I'm so bored when I do it, it's like I'm not even there."

"Mm-hmm," I said. And then, because I sounded like a bitch to my own ears, I said, "Uh, you look like you hardly ever need to do anything in the first place." It seemed like a nice thing to say. I thought she was too skinny, to tell you the truth.

She smiled and stared at me. She had these huge, blue, Barbie-doll-looking eyes. A lot of her was Barbie-doll-looking. I'm not saying that's bad. I'm just saying.

"I like your body better," she said. "I'd kill for your ass."

That was nice, what she said. I finally smiled at her for real. "Yeah, well. Tell Bobby that."

"I did."

I pretended I didn't hear her.

"*Bobby*," she said, after a second. Like *please*. "He shouldn't have to be told something so obvious."

I didn't like her talking about Bobby with that tone. But still, what she said had a ring of truth to it.

"Listen," Amber said. She had a nice voice, soft but sure of her-self. "Do you . . . would you like . . . I would love it if we could maybe grab a bite to eat."

I looked around the gym. "With Bobby?"

"No. Not with Bobby."

"Oh," I said.

I felt funny. The thing was, Amber was okay and all that. Even if she looked fake, she wasn't. There was something down home about her. Never thought I'd say that. I talked trash about her for the longest. But a couple of days before, I saw her do something. She'd gotten in this big dude's face about leaving the StairMaster all sweaty and disgusting. *Did he think his mother was going to come clean up his filth?* she'd asked. *Or did he expect one of us other women to clean his shit, before we got to do our own workouts?* He'd called her a bitch, but he'd wiped it off like she'd asked. Amber wasn't playing with that fool. I liked that. Lunch with her was something different, though.

"I don't know," I said. "Maybe next time? I kind of want to get home." I did want to get home, even though I didn't really have anything to do once I got there. I just kept seeing Bobby's face, cheesing it up, ecstatic that Amber and I were going to lunch, like he was one number away from winning the lottery.

"Oh," she said. "Okay." She stared at me some more but looked down at her shoes after a second. When she looked up again, she had a little halfhearted smile.

"Real soon, though," I said. Don't ask me why I did this, but I touched her shoulder.

"Next time, then," Amber said, and then she walked away. "Next time" sounded like a contract.

LATER, AT HOME TAKING a shower, I turned on the radio real loud, since Bobby wasn't home to have a fit about it. I played music to make me want to dance. Evelyn "Champagne" King. *Champagne.* I liked her attitude. *Got to be real, got to be real.* It was music that I used to dance to when I worked at the Eight Ball. Thinking about being real, Amber came to mind. Every time I saw her, I kept expecting her to get all giggly and white-girl silly over Bobby. Or just be slutty. Everybody else did. But she looked like she could take or leave Bobby. Mostly leave, and keep on stepping. That just made Bobby get even more stupid over her. Amber this and Amber that. I half-wished she'd hit on Bobby so he'd shut up.

Taking a shower was the best part of working out. I stood there and let the water massage my body, little warm needles with dull points. I started laughing out of nowhere, because I remembered this time when me and Bobby decided to smoke some weed and drink about two bottles of red wine.

Bobby had eaten like food was going out of style, but I hadn't eaten a bite because I was trying to be all skinny and dainty and cute and shit. Bobby was on top of me, covering my whole body, practically. He was being extra sweet, extra slow, saying my name in a voice I heard less and less lately. I was hypnotized. High, too. "La Donna," Bobby whispered, and he put his tongue in my ear. Right then, I got sick to my stomach. I jumped up, had to balance myself on the edge of Bobby's futon couch.

"Where's your bathroom?" I moaned.

"What?" Bobby was confused—and hard. "What's wrong with you?"

"I don't feel too good," I said. Bobby only had a studio, so the bathroom was just three steps away. I thought I could make it. Bobby's apartment was practically all white or cream colored. That was a shame. I did make it into the bathroom, but it didn't matter, because I threw up red all over Bobby's clean white bathroom, all over his pomade and creams and ten bottles of cologne. I stayed in there for what seemed like days and months and a lifetime before Bobby knocked and came in without an answer from me. I was on my knees, holding on to the toilet like it was my long-lost friend.

To his credit, Bobby didn't say a word—at first. He just looked at all the red covering every single thing in his bathroom. I hadn't known him long, but I already knew he was the kind of guy who turned a book back to the *exact* position it was in before he picked it up from his table. Bobby only had two books in his house: *His Way*—Frank Sinatra's biography—and *How to Train Your Dog*. But still.

"Are you fuckin kiddin me?" he said finally. "You okay? What the hell?"

"Yeah," I said. "No."

"Lemme look at you." Bobby pulled my braids from my face and grabbed a towel from a rack. He wiped all the vomit from my face. "Can you stand up?"

"Yeah." I lifted my head. "There," I said.

"Fuck," Bobby said. He stood me up, leaned me on the sink, and started undressing me. "You gotta get cleaned up. Lemme clean you up."

Somehow, he got me in the shower, bathed me, dried me off, put a T-shirt and socks on me, laid me down on the bed, and pulled the covers over me. Before I passed out, I saw Bobby working in the bathroom with the mop and pail. The same bathroom I was standing in now. I had to remember that whenever I wanted to smack Bobby with him getting on me about everything and nothing at all.

I turned off the shower, dried off, and looked at myself in the mirror. I thought I looked okay; everything did except the tits. I'd gotten them done a couple of years ago, when I thought I was supposed to look like all the other strippers with big tits—except I was big all over. I should have known that I'd never look like the skinny white girls, unless I stopped eating, and fuck that. They never ended up feeling like a part of my body, these tits. They were from some other place. But maybe Bobby was right, and Amber was wrong. Bobby could fit a whole inch of my fat in between his fingers when he pinched me, and I didn't want to hear it. I could at least tighten up here and there. Cut down.

•

I RAN OUT OF creative ways to blow off Amber. Every time I saw her, she came at me, asking to have a coffee or lunch, like it was the first time she'd asked me, like I hadn't said, "No, I can't," five times before. So we grabbed a coffee, because lunch seemed like getting in too deep. Once you start eating with somebody, it's hard to get away from them. If I couldn't stand her, I wanted to be able to get up out of there right quick.

Having coffee with Amber made me nervous, like going out on a date. Small stuff was always on my mind, like who would get to the door of the coffee shop first, and who would open it? Was she going to offer to pay for my latte, but why would she though, since it wasn't a date? Would I trip over my own feet? And was she checking out my body when I walked in front of her? Bobby said she'd mentioned the shape of it more than once. I'd never been nervous around no white girl before, and it felt weird to be jumpy and jittery.

We walked around the corner to some small place, and she *wouldn't* let me pay for my own coffee. When I put my money down, she said, "Please, let me. For the pleasure of your company," and she smiled at me. She had two deep dimples in both cheeks that I never noticed before. She said, "Why don't you find a place for us to sit? I'll wait for the coffee and come to you." So that's what I did. My eyes skimmed over everybody reading their papers and typing on their laptops. In a minute, I saw that the coffees were ready, and she came over to me, already talking.

"Did you know that *La Donna* means 'the woman' in Italian?" She slid into her chair and pushed my coffee toward me. "*The* woman, not even *a*. Like, there are no other women." She grinned at me, showing teeth just as white and perfect as Bobby's. Then her lips closed over them real slow while she stared at me.

"No, I didn't know it meant that in Italian. I think my mama just liked the way it sounded." I was having trouble looking her in the eye, so I looked around the café and stared at some other tiny white girl who was talking too loud on her cell phone about her doctor's appointment.

"Don't you hate how everyone's always on the phone everywhere you go now?" Amber said, following my eyes. "Like we really want to hear about her shrink's advice or whatever she's talking about."

"I know," I said, because it was all I could think to say. The other tiny woman flipped her blond ponytail and propped her feet up on the table. I thought about how she was making herself at home, taking up space and filling up everybody's ears, as small as she was. I thought about how my mama would smack me for putting my feet up on somebody's table, especially in public. She kept me in check, my mama. *I don't care if you are grown,* she was always saying. Looked like nobody had ever checked this girl before in her life.

"What does *Amber* mean?" I finally asked, hoping that would get her to stop staring at me so hard.

"Well," she started, running her thin fingers over the top of her coffee cup, "I don't know what it *means,* but I know that amber is this stuff that comes from trees from millions of years ago—"

"I know," I said. "It was this liquid that, like, oozed out of the trees and trapped all kinds of stuff in it, like twigs and bugs . . . all kinds of stuff it picked up along the way. It got hard and turned into stone." Amber's mouth was open and she was squinting her eyes like she was having trouble seeing me. "I just thought maybe *Amber* meant something else. I don't know why I was thinking that." I kind of laughed at myself and took a sip of my coffee. Amber reached across the table and touched my wrist, real light, with just the tip of her finger.

"Hey, I forgot. You probably know all about this kind of stuff. You're always reading those astrology books and stuff at the gym."

"Astronomy. Astronomy's different. From astrology. And from rocks and stuff."

"I know. I meant *astronomy*. I'm just saying. I shouldn't have talked like you didn't know what amber was."

"That's okay," I said. I was thinking about her touching me on my wrist. She'd touched me once before, and this time I could still feel her finger there, like a warm spot. I remembered something else I knew about amber. "You know how you can tell fake amber from real amber?

Amber shrugged.

"I learned this once: If you rub real amber with something, it'll turn electric, but plastic fake stuff that's supposed to be real doesn't feel as warm, and it doesn't feel electric."

Amber leaned into the table, put her elbows on it, and then put her face on her knuckles. "Bobby's real lucky you're his girlfriend," she said. She sat up straight and then pulled at her feet so she was sitting cross-legged in her chair. "And I know you probably think it's weird that I would want to have coffee or lunch with you, but I think you're just beautiful, and I would love it if we could get to know each other better, because I love beautiful, smart women." She took the little paper thing from around the cup that keeps you from burning your hands when your drink is hot and started ripping it into little pieces, just staring at me. She was the worst about that staring, like you were a meal and she was starving.

Something about her made me like her, even though she made me feel weird, too. Before, I used to think she was just a silly blond little white girl, like the one who was *still* talking on her cell phone a few tables over. But there was something real about Amber, even if her lips were fake, her hair color was fake, and all kinds of parts of her body were fake. Maybe it was just that she told me I was beautiful in a tone I hadn't heard from Bobby in a month of Sundays. Or maybe it was because she said I was smart, matter-of-fact, wasn't being funny about it, believed it. Whatever it was, I felt so weird that I wanted to leave. I looked at my watch and then back at Amber, who looked sad.

"I shouldn't have said what I said."

"No," I said. "What you said was nice, really." And then before I really thought about it, I said, "Maybe we could go out sometime, get to know each other better." We laughed about some of the people at the gym for a little while, and then she told me about how she was a composer, wrote music—and who would have thought that? I took one last sip of my coffee before I stood up. "I should go, though. Bobby's waiting for me back at the gym to give him a ride home."

"Okay." She gave me a weak smile and stood up. She came closer to me. "Mind if I give you a hug before we go?" I wanted to make her feel better, like things weren't weird. So I hugged her first. And I gave her a real hug, I held on for a long second. When we pulled away from each other, she gave me one of those big toothy grins.

"You're a good hugger," she said.

"That's what Bobby says," I said.

"Hmm," she said, like *Bobby, who? Like I give a shit.* Then she turned to leave the café.

Driving Bobby home, I was tired. It was hot, the air conditioning was busted, and traffic was working my nerves almost as much as Bobby.

"So, okay. Wait. She buys you the coffee, and then you guys sit down, and then what?"

"*Nothing.* We just talked." In the car ahead of us, some kid, a boy it looked like, was waving at us from the backseat. I waved back. When I did, though, he gave me the middle finger.

"Motherfucker," I said, my voice high. I flipped the kid off.

"Whoa! Hey!" Bobby said. "A kid and everything. *Nice.*"

I rolled my eyes. "They ought to do something with this street. This is ridiculous."

"She ask you out again? What?"

"*Bobby.*"

"C'mon. *Bobby*. Did she or didn't she?" Bobby bit down on his knuckles.

"You should have drove," I said. Everything about everything bothered me. The kid in front of us was waving something at us now, a goddamn doll. He kept flipping me off and waving it, and Bobby kept running his mouth about the three of us fucking, and I couldn't breathe in that hot-ass Mustang anymore.

"Fuck!" I yelled, and I banged my hand on the steering wheel. "Fuck!"

"What I tell you?" Bobby said. He thumped me hard on the thigh. "What is your *problem*?"

HE WAS WANTING TO know what I wanted for our anniversary. "A whole year with me, sweetheart. Paradise or what, huh?"

"Or what."

"All right, smart-ass. See? Try and be nice to somebody—"

"I'm just playin!" I stood behind him and hugged him tight.

"Seriously, though," Bobby said. "I want to do something nice for you." He turned and faced me. He kissed me on the forehead.

"I don't know. Maybe just a romantic dinner? Here even. Make me something special, just for me."

"I don't know how to make no chitlins or collard greens or whatever the fuck."

"Well, I don't want none of that weird Greek health shit you're always trying to give me." I pinched him on the side.

"Ow! Bitch." He laughed. "Okay, how bout I take you out, spend a couple of bucks on you. Some place nice."

"And I can eat any kind of fattening thing I want without hearing it from you."

"Fine," Bobby said. "I'll hook you up nice, baby."

"Better hook me up nice."

He squeezed me hard, tighter and tighter until I screamed at him, laughing. "Stop, Bobby! Stop! I mean it!"

WE WENT TO A place kind of far from where we lived, a place that's gone now. It was Aunt Kizzy's Back Porch in the Marina. I ordered fried chicken, collard greens, macaroni and cheese, and corn bread. Bobby tried to come between me and my macaroni and cheese, but I wouldn't let him. I was feeling good, had a buzz on from the wine we were drinking. All the planets were lined up right, even though Professor Salazar said talk like that was astrology. A world of difference from what he was trying to teach us.

"Happy anniversary, baby," I said. I fed him a bite.

"Hmm, this is good," he said. "How come you never make this for me?"

"What? And hear fat this and fat that? Gimme a break."

"Well, you're right about that. You like my choice, though? A couple of people at the gym said this would be a good place."

I nodded and smiled at him bright. "It's good, Bobby." Really, it was just okay. "You know that Jamaican place in Leimert Park? That would have been good, too." It would have been a *lot* better. It was in a black neighborhood where they didn't have no marinas.

"Never heard of it." Bobby shook his leg under the table. He was being jittery and distracted all during dinner. Biting his nails, jiggling his leg, and playing with his hair.

"What's wrong with you?" I worked on my peach cobbler.

"Nothing," Bobby said. He lifted our wine bottle off the table to show the waiter we needed another bottle of wine. He smiled and winked at me.

"Member the time," I took a drink from my glass, "that time I threw up in your bathroom?"

"Christ, La Donna, you gotta bring that up now?" He nodded at my wineglass. "Better slow down with that."

"That was funny, though, Bobby. Almost a year ago. Can you believe it?"

"Yeah, funny to you."

I put my fork down and pushed my plate away some. Bobby took my fork and finished off my pie. "That was sweet, though, Bobby. How you cleaned me up, cleaned up everything." I leaned into the table, trying to get as close to him as I could. I thought I was the luckiest woman sitting with the finest man in the whole place. I felt so close to Bobby, so happy, I was thinking he must have been feeling it, way across the table, me shining everything on him.

"What," he said. "Like I had a choice."

I was smiling at Bobby before, but I stopped. "What do you mean? Course you had a choice."

"If you think I was gonna let my bathroom stay vomity, you're crazy, and if you think I'm gonna let a vomity woman sleep passed out next to me, you're even more crazy."

I hadn't ever thought of it like that. A cloud passed over my face.

Bobby looked at me. "Don't start."

I looked around the restaurant and sank down in my chair.

"Come on. Don't get mad. Come here."

I sat still.

"Come here," Bobby said. When I ignored him, he said, "All right. I thought it was kind of cute, you puking all over my god-damn bathroom. The cutest, sexiest shit I ever saw."

I tried not to smile at that, but Bobby could be funny sometimes. He saw me trying not to smile.

"Lemme kiss you, and then I'll tell you your surprise."

I sat up straight. Hard to do after my fourth glass of wine. "What surprise?"

"I ain't gonna tell you till you kiss me."

I did. "Well?"

"Okay," Bobby cracked his knuckles and then took both my hands. "I got something waiting for you back home."

"What? What, Bobby? What is it?" I got happy, got rid of that cloud real fast. I knew it was that telescope I'd pointed out to Bobby one day when we were shopping. It cost a fortune—a fortune to me and Bobby, but if he'd been thinking about me at all this year, even a little bit, he would have been saving up for it. I'd dragged him into the shop and pointed it out to him, plain and obvious. He said I must have wanted to blow my teacher; that was the only reason I'd be so into the "most boring shit on the planet. The fuckin stripping astrologist. That's funny," Bobby had said.

"Astronomy," I had said.

He'd turned down the corners of his mouth and shrugged. "Whatever."

But maybe he'd just been trying to throw me off the trail. "You got me that telescope, didn't you?" I said it like I was accusing him of something and happy to bust him.

Bobby stopped grinning. "Wha? Nah. I didn't get you any fuckin telescope. This is better. Way better."

My heart started beating real fast, and my hands started shaking. Bobby had gotten me a ring. "It's a ring!" I screamed. Some folks in the restaurant turned to look at us.

"What? A *ring*," Bobby said, blowing out of his nose. "That's funny. Wow," he said, shaking his head.

I blinked and frowned at him. I was confused. "Then what? What'd you get me?"

Bobby looked into my eyes. Serious. He glanced over his shoulder before he leaned into me as close as he could. He smiled. "Okay, don't freak out."

"Yeah?" I smiled back at him.

"At home? Right now? I got Amber waiting for you."

"Amber?" I was still confused. "What for?"

"What *for*," Bobby said. "Don't be cute."

My hands were in Bobby's. I squeezed his hands as hard as I could, letting everything he was telling me find a place to settle in my head. "You're telling me," I took a deep breath, "that Amber. Amber from the gym. She's in our apartment. Waiting for us. For all of us to have sex."

"That's right," Bobby said, hopeful, kind of holding his breath.

"That's your present. To me. My anniversary present."

I didn't know whether to cry or punch Bobby in his perfect actor face. I couldn't look him in the eye, because I was afraid I'd cry, which would have made me real pissed at myself.

"It's *part* of your present." He reached into his jacket pocket in the chair next to us.

Bastard. He was just playing. He handed me a long velvet box. When I snapped it open, there was a shiny gold chain in it, with a little white stone attached to it.

"You like it? I got you this, too. It's a moonstone. I told the guy at the place what you liked, and he said this, you'd like." Bobby looked like he was really wanting me to like his present, but I couldn't fake it.

I turned the stone over in my hand. It was beautiful and felt cool in my palm. "*Too?*" I said finally. "So you're not kidding about the Amber stuff."

"Uh-uh," Bobby said.

I held the chain in my hands. Amber was in my apartment. Bobby asked her to be there. Or did she ask?

"Ah, fuck. I shouldn't of told you," Bobby said. "I should of just got you home. See what happened when you got there."

"You should have seen." My voice had no life in it. "You're really fucking crazy, Bobby. You know that?"

"What? You said you were down, might try this someday."

"I was just *playing*. I wasn't for *real*."

"Then why'd you say all that stuff then?"

"I was just half-kidding!"

"What half, Donna?" Bobby was yelling. "And we got Amber waiting there and everything . . . She's going to feel really shitty about this. I told her it would work out."

I poured myself more wine, shook my head slow and careful.

Bobby threw up his hands. They dropped down loud on his thighs. "She's supposed to be waiting in the closet. I'm supposed to call, and she's supposed to get in the closet when we get there, and I'm supposed to put a blindfold on you, get all sexy and loose with you, and that's when we were going to surprise you."

I put my head in both my hands and coughed out a laugh.

"Then what am I supposed to tell Amber?" he asked.

"What do I care, Bobby? Tell her whatever you want. You did that already. She can stay in the closet all night."

Bobby's eyes followed people leaving the restaurant. "We gotta tell her something, Donna. It ain't nice."

"It ain't nice, Donna," I said in a deep, fake Bobby voice.

"You're fuckin drunk," he said. He saw the waiter and then motioned for the check. "And you better not get sick in the car."

I FELL ASLEEP ON the way home. I was full of wine and food. I felt heavy. I didn't dream about stuff, nothing at all. I stayed asleep until we got off the freeway. You always do that, stay asleep when you're riding, until you get off the freeway. Something about going so fast, the sound of the air *swooshing* by, like floating, being in a trance. But then, when you feel the car slowing down, going down the off-ramp, you feel some kind of change, something about the ride feels different, even if you're in a deep sleep, dreaming. You wake up.

WE WERE IN THE garage of the apartment building. The building
was on Franklin, shitty, the stucco all stained and peeling, but all
the cars in the garage were nice.

"Hey," Bobby said. He touched me face. "You all right? You not
sick or nothing? You can get out, right?"

I nodded. Bobby came around and helped me out. He was trying
to be nice.

"Didn't you say there was going to be one of those eclipses
today?" He put his arms around me and walked to the elevator.

"It wasn't that great," I said. Bobby pushed the UP button, and we
got in and went up. Earlier that day, I'd spent a half hour standing
outside. I put a hole in a piece of paper, turned my back to the sun,
and looked down on the sidewalk while all the cars sped by me
on the street. I saw a little bitty shadowy thing that looked like a
moon with a bright light all around the edges. It wasn't as cool as
Professor Salazar said. But he said we had to see it that way, with
the filter and everything, or else we'd burn the shit out of our eyes.
He didn't say "shit," but he said we really, really didn't want to look
straight at the eclipse or else we could really hurt ourselves.

I wasn't drunk—*as* drunk—as I was at the restaurant. I thought
of Amber waiting for me in the apartment, and I thought it would
be nice to see her.

The elevator bell rang when we got to our floor. When we got
to our apartment, Bobby put his key in the door and looked at me
before he turned it.

"I don't care," I said, which was the truth. Being with Amber
sounded better than being alone with Bobby just then. She would
look at me like she really wanted me, like she knew what I was, and
I wanted that.

Bobby opened the door, and I went to the couch. I started taking off all my clothes. Bobby, too. He stood in front of me and put a scarf around my eyes. There was a little slash I could still see through, so I squeezed my eyes shut. I still wasn't sure how far I was going to go, even if I was already in the middle of it, anyway. I lay down on the carpet. Bobby didn't want the lights off. He wanted to be able to see everything; but me, I wasn't supposed to be able to tell when Bobby stopped touching me and when Amber started.

I knew right away, though. Amber's hands were light and smooth. They moved all over my hips and breasts, between my legs. Warm, soft hands, gentle hands that felt like liquid. Her hands were so warm I felt tingly, like I was on fire. I still had the blindfold on, but when I looked through the little slash, I saw Amber on her hands and knees between me and Bobby. Amber felt good, but she didn't come close enough to what I wanted. I wanted how Bobby used to make me feel. I wanted something bigger than me. I could sort of make out Bobby moving slow behind Amber, like a shadow. "You like that, Sunshine? You like that?" he was whispering to me. But I didn't feel like sunshine, not like I usually did when he called me that. Bobby thought the three of us together in that room was big, a big thing that would take his mind off Louie. But he was still trapped, doing without seeing. And now, there was something, *somebody* between us. I was in it, seeing it. Me and him and Amber wasn't half as good as he talked about it being. I was disappointed in everybody and everything. But at least I could finally see clear.

NOW, IN THE NOT QUITE DARK

Even before the dead girl in the water tower, Dean has been haunted. And ever since his girl threw a cliché at him, the one about space and needing it, there's been a feeling: If he reaches out his hand, waves it around in front of him like a blind man, he's going to want to think that there is someone out there. A tether. "I'm gone," his girl had said. "But I'll always think of you." And she moved on like people do, leaving the scent of her hair, he swears, in the walls, in the sheets, no matter how many times he's washed them. She has a point, his girl. His mother appreciated his sensitivity when he was a child; he was the kind of kid who cried after complete strangers left him. What are you *crying* for? His father would beg to know. You just *met* so-and-so. It'd be some guy from his father's office who'd come over to the house for a drink, some lady that was nice to him in the waiting room of Nordstrom while his mother tried on clothes, her legs the only thing visible in the changing room, which set him off, too. When are they coming back? He'd weep, snot running over his lip. Hurry up, Mama. Come out. Come out!

Everywhere, ghosts. The longer he lives Downtown, the more years that pass—and now it is eight—the more he is haunted. At first, it's a vague curiosity, not quite a haunting. At first, when he moves into his loft eight years in the past, he reads the directory from an unknown year in the lobby of his building, built in 1905, with the condescending wonder of a person in the present looking at the past. He will never be in the past. The names! You can almost see the people belonging to those names, who used to live and work in the Pacific Electric Building, originally the Huntington, in the waves that people talk about, when they talk about the waves of immigrants who made their way to Los Angeles. Look at this, he always says, showing off to visitors the directory of names almost as long as the journey that had brought the men to 610 South Main Street a long, long time ago. The syllables in their names rising up and down were enough to make you feel seasick: Tzschentke. Niedzwiecki, Uszerowicz, Margolotti, Rambukwella. And Lopez. M. Lopez had worked or lived in Dean's apartment, number 307, some time a long, long time ago. They were Polish, Sri Lankan, Italian, and Mexican. Dean looked it up. He wanted to be sure about these people once their ghosts started haunting him, the distance between him and them feeling smaller and smaller. They were waves, their names were waves, and now Dean in his refurbished loft was a part of a wave of people coming in with their dogs wearing shoes, drinking cocktails created at the hands of mixologists. He drank Hemingways, Old Fashioneds, a nice bourbon or a blended Scotch if he had a few extra bucks. Vodka, *screwdrivers* were for dumbfucks, for people who didn't know any better.

So that's how the neighborhood, the Historic Core, was changing. A Ross had popped up on Broadway. A Starbucks on Spring. People pushing strollers with babies in them, not just belongings, blankets, food, and all the rest. That was the vibe when Dean had first moved

Downtown, when he was closer to twenty, not thirty. The West was still wild and he had felt like a pioneer. It was rough, heroin needles, human feces, prostitution rough. No covered wagon packed with his belongings, but he had had an empty building that was almost entirely his and one hundred other people's. The building held 314 units, now all full, but then, he could stand in his hallway and hear echoes and more echoes of his own voice, and he freaked himself out thinking about the voices of those who had been around since 1905. But this feeling of voices being heard, of echoes, was not altogether freaky. Dean felt settled and unsettled at the same time. He walked around with something heavy in his stomach most days, waiting for good surprises and bad ones, waiting to finally meet his expectation, waiting for this thing to be born.

But before Main Street had changed on Dean, it had changed on so many others before him, people who had lived there for years before he'd even heard of Downtown and so now he feels like an ass for resenting Starbucks—the Starbucks he goes to every day, even with the occasional junkie nodding off at a table or shooting up in the bathroom. He's embarrassed for the Dean who is closer to twenty, rather than thirty, trying to hold back change. It's like looking back on the person he was even longer ago, the person who had to let everyone know that he had heard of this band or that band before anyone else had ever heard of them. *That* guy. He knows now that there is always someone who has come before you, someone who is going to come after. And they do, they have, the people who want to live Downtown, see Downtown. They come to the hotel next door now called Stay on Main, even though it will always be known as Hotel Cecil, but if they checked the oh-hell-no reviews online they would know better.

And, so, now there was this girl found on the roof of the Hotel Cecil, just two buildings down. Disappeared at first, then dead, inevitably. But before her, in his own building, there was a guy who fell to his death out of his window on the fifth floor, jacked up on weed and alcohol. And then there was the other guy, also on the fifth floor (goddamn that was an unlucky floor), who shot himself in the head and who had, by extension, murdered his Chihuahua when he forgot to—or hell, maybe dude even meant to do it— leave food and water for it after he was no longer alive to take care of it. The insult to the self-injury was that on the day the guy's body was discovered, *CSI: New York* had been filming in the building, all the time a stand-in for some kind of New York–looking building, and so the story was not that a man had shot himself in the head and gone ignored for nearly five weeks, the late-rent notices taped to his door getting thicker and more collage-like by the weeks, tenants mistaking the smell of his decaying body for the smell of gunk trapped in the trash shoot. No, the real story was that an actor named Gary Sinise was in the building, filming a show about death, when there was an actual dead guy on the set of the fake New York building. Ironic! Dean had seen a coroner's van parked in front of the building that day, thought *bummer* for the dead person, but then, relief: The van said *New York Coroner*. It was a fake death, a TV death. Except it wasn't, the way it all went down. They explained it all on the news, all about Gary Sinise, except they never said the name of the dead guy. The deceased. The person most tenants hadn't heard of. Only Gary Sinise, Gary Sinise. A name that lasts, that everybody knows, but nobody knows for how long.

The dead girl was a tourist, from Canada, and like so many other tourists, she'd come Downtown because now—again—it was the place to be.

DEAN AND HIS MOTHER sit on the roof of Pacific Electric Lofts, the first skyscraper in Los Angeles and once the biggest building, too. Trains, Red Cars, used to thread themselves in and out of the building, onto the streets, in and out and throughout the city like arteries pushing through life's blood. His mother, he knows, prefers anywhere that's nowhere near the street, even his perfectly fine seven-hundred-square-foot apartment on the third floor is dangerously close to the muck below. Every time, the same questions. Why does her son live on such a dirty street, Skid Row a stone's throw away? In one room? Facing other folks' apartments and those facing his, just looking in on his business like he's putting on a show? She used to hold her nose from the minute she pulled into the parking garage until she burst through the roof doors and took in the scent of kumquats, roses, and just a little bit of piss from the Astroturf dog run just below the pool deck. But her attitude about Dean's choices has improved, if not changed. Downtown is nice now. Well, nicer. She doesn't mind telling folks that this is where her son lives.

"I'm glad we're up here instead of sitting inside your apartment like a couple of fish in a bowl," she says, wiggling her short body up and up until she's properly stretched out on the deck chair and settled with her wine in hand.

The lap pool shimmers, and the hot tub gurgles. His mother closes her eyes with her hands clasped around the cup of wine at her chest. Dean imagines her lying in a coffin, but he pushes the image out of his head. She's fine. She's here. She's come to check on her lovesick boy. That's her story. But the older she gets, the more she seems to be looking for him, and not his father, who most everybody knew was screwing as many women as possible to keep himself out of the ground. Somebody's dog in one of the penthouses is yapping endlessly for company, but his family has likely gone and left him all alone. "Poor baby," Dean's mother says. "Nobody likes to be alone."

His mother has mentioned a show. He wants to tell his mother about the time he did put on a show, his business hanging out for anyone across the way to see, though at night and for a lot of the day most people closed the curtains on their lives. The guy across the way, a smoker who liked to hang out of his window with a towel around his waist, was having a party, a loud three-in-the-morning party. For years now, they had been waving at each other from their windows, and sometimes the guy would nod goodbye after flicking his butt out of the window, which Dean hated, before turning to disappear into the shadows of his apartment. Dean had pulled open the curtains, lifted his floor-to-ceiling window, and stood there naked. "Yo! Yo, motherfucker! A brother is trying to sleep over here!" A crowd stood in front of the window across the way, pointing and laughing, but Dean was too pissed to care. "All right!" A woman wearing cat ears, for some reason, leaned out of the window. "All right! We see you! We hear you! Put your dick away!" she hollered. A moment later, the music was lowered, and Dean had fallen asleep thinking about the civility of it all. Eight years that guy was across the way, and one day he was gone; an older gray-haired dude who never says boo lives across the way now. He misses towel guy. He thinks, I never got a chance to say goodbye. But then he thinks, *Get a grip, man.* You didn't even know that guy.

"I like my windows," Dean says. "It's like *Rear Window.*" But his mother has never seen that movie, and the windows in this building with their curtains mostly closed only fluttered with the suggestion of the lives going on behind them. Nothing like *Rear Window.* They're never wide open at night, enough to see murder, mayhem, the toke or sip or sleep of a person slowly passing into history. He looks, though. All the time. Just in case.

"No," his mother says. "This is the best thing about this building, the pool." She takes a sip of chardonnay from her plastic cup. Glass is not allowed. Something about the pool and glass being difficult to clean out of it and, Dean is certain, lawsuits. His mother is not a drinker, not by a sight. The wine is Dean's idea. He means to paint

a picture for his mother, to make her visit nice. California. Los Angeles. Swimming pools on rooftops. And wine, even in plastic cups,
wine on a rooftop, the sun shining down on them on a Saturday
afternoon like grace. It doesn't get any better. The rest of the building's charms are lost on her. Seriously cool stuff. The dark hallways,
the gray veins of the chalk-white marble stretching and entangled in
paths impossible to trace, like they're pumping blood in and through
the building. The doorways out of detective film noir, silhouettes
looming large against the glass and then shrinking as they pass by.
"That would scare the hell out of me every time," his mother had
said, the first time she sat on his Ikea loveseat and faced the door.
"It looks like somebody is coming to get you. I don't like people all
around, on top, and up under me like that." But, this is how people
are supposed to live, together, side-by-side, rooms on top of rooms.
This is what it means to live in the city. More scary: The houses
stretched out in rows, a family and then another family and then
another family in rows, abandoned bikes on uneven, yellow-green
lawns, nobody on the streets, day or night, like some post-
apocalyptic scene from a zombie movie. He is coming up on thirty,
but he is still too young for that. He's still more willing to take the
dog shit in the hallways, the drummer next door, the bloody tampon
in the stairwell he found that time (he did not *even* want to know,
and yet, what the fuck?), and the morons who set the trash down
outside the trash chute, instead of just putting that shit *in* the chute.

The light has shifted, and his mother relaxes into the brown
trying-for-deco lounge chair. She kicks off her white Keds and stares
over the rooftop and smiles, caught up in the glamour of six o'clock
sunshine. "If this was all yours, this would be perfect," she says. "If
you were all by yourself. This rooftop is out of a magazine. Perfect."

"But it's not all mine," Dean says. He leans back in his chair
and shades his eyes from the glare bouncing off his horn-rimmed
glasses. "It's why I like it, that it's not all mine."

"And that's why your ass will always be broke," his mother says. "People who rent are throwing their money away, I'm telling you. A waste of time and money. Buy. A. House."

"I'm not broke," Dean says. When his mother says nothing, he says, "I'm not *broke*. But I'm not buying a house." He has the feeling he had when he was a boy, the feeling that grown folks were stupid, though now he was a grown folk, like the time he tried to tell his mother that somebody was hiding under his bed when he was a kid. No, no, his mother had said. Go back to sleep. But somebody *was*. One of their neighbors, this kid named Sippy, teenage and always with a soda like a baby with his bottle, always dirty as hell and silent like a mute, had come in and crawled under the bed and fallen asleep. "I told you. I told you, Mama!" Dean had yelled, running around their small apartment like he'd just won something. "I told you!" And he laughed because his mother didn't know what she was talking about and because Sippy wasn't even scary now that they knew Sippy was there. Had been there. His father had not been home, again, of course, but they were not alone, the two of them —the three of them. His mother had screamed like Sippy was the boogieman and pulled him out from under the bed. Chased him out. That was more than twenty years ago. Now, Dean wants to know. Where are you, Sippy?

"Do you remember Sippy Brown?"

"*Who?*"

"Sippy Brown."

His mother puts her almost-finished wine down on the concrete and spreads her hands. "His crazy ass? Just made himself at home," she says, and shakes her head, picks up her cup. She laughs, sudden like a sneeze, and shakes her head again. "Good old Sippy. Nutty as a fruitcake." She is quiet for a moment, lost in Sippy, before she gets back to her hot topic.

She goes through her usual list: If you're going to have a girlfriend, a wife, a family, you're not going to be able to stay down here forever, no matter how much you want to. And anyway, you should have bought a place when you were first down here, when stuff was really cheap. You waited too long, and now, you're going to have to pay house prices for apartment living. You can't afford that. It's too bad, now that it's prime housing. Now that it's all cleaned up and nice.

And by "all cleaned up," she means of *people*.

Dean *had* made some nice changes at the start-up where he worked. They developed apps to maximize advertising capabilities for companies; apps that basically made it easier for companies to stalk people. Everyone wants you until you're gone. He opens his mouth to say he could buy a loft here, Downtown, but then closes it. Shit is *expensive*. As if you could truly own any of this in the first place. Dean looks out over the rooftops, at the don't-fuck-with-me griffin perched on top of one of the buildings across the way.

"Keep tabs, my brother," Dean says.

His mother says, "What?"

"Nothing," Dean says. "Look at that gargoyle over there. The griffin. He's got the body of a lion and the face of an eagle. Look at those wings. He's like, 'Yo, this is my city, fools. I'm watching you. I will always be watching you.'"

"Don't say that!" his mother says, and she shivers. "Let me enjoy my rooftop view, without all that weird mess."

"The king of all creatures. He'll be here in concrete, long after us."

His mother raises an eyebrow at him. *Stop*, her eyes say. *I mean it*. And then she asks him. How much does he think the building is worth?

•

SHE DOESN'T MUCH CARE for the building, the guts of it, but the roof with a view. That's what really matters, to her. Picture-perfect, the roof. Out of a magazine. But looking over at the roof of The Cecil, Dean can't help himself. He's got to bring up the dead girl. She's right in front of them, even though they can't see her. She was floating in a water tank. Now she's not. But Dean can't look at the roof of The Cecil ever again, ever, ever, without thinking, there she was. Is. Elisa Lam. Like Tzschentke, Niedzwiecki, her life brings her to California, to L.A., to Downtown, to Main Street, and then leaves her here.

He starts talking, his tone low and careful, like a troop leader around a late-night campfire. But the sun is blaring, bouncing and glinting off indeterminate sources of light all around them, as if fighting for its life. *I will not go down. I will never set.* "That's the tank where that woman was found dead," he says.

"Do not," his mother says, "talk about that."

"But it is."

"But that's already in the past," his mother says. "That's already over. Why keep talking about it? Poor girl."

"No," Dean says. "For real, though. People trying to brush their teeth, take showers. Can you even imagine? You think, low water pressure, okay. It's an old building. Whatever. What're you going to do?" He shrugs. "But then, you find out that the water in your mouth, that you're showering with, in that water are the cells, the invisible things that make up a human being. You're covered in ghost."

"Is this why Brandy left you? Because you're sounding weird right now."

"It's not weird. Just true."

"Truly *off*."

"But it's better than just being put in the ground, I think. Now she's everywhere. Hitched a ride with whoever had some water those days at The Cecil. I think it's comforting, no?"

"No. You're sounding like you got some Sippy in you right now. Let's go, Sippy," his mother says. She looks like Frankenstein, rising out of her lounge chair, stiff and aimless. "Your Afro is flat in the back," she says, reaching over to pick at his hair like he's five. She reaches down to retrieve her empty plastic cup, and Dean takes in his mother, her white Keds, white jeans, and white T-shirt imbued with the orange of the sinking sun, like an image caught in sepia tone. She fluffs her hair, more and more streaked with gray, cut in a bob like a girl from nine decades before. "You killed my vibe," she says. "All the dead people and lions with bird heads. I'm ready to get out of here."

THEY DECIDE TO GO downstairs for one last drink before his mother makes the drive back to the San Fernando Valley, to sit outside the restaurant and enjoy the fading light. They take the elevator, and when Dean steps in after his mother, she's still facing the mirror, fluffing her hair, and she catches his eyes. "Who *are* you?" she asks. "All those tattoos. Where did my baby go?" He stares at their reflections in the mirror. He's so much taller than she is, and he remembers far and away being knee-high and pulling on her pants leg, missing her while she says, *I haven't gone anywhere. Don't you see me standing here?* "Your baby's a grown-ass man," Dean says, and he traces his and his mother's initials into the red velvet of the elevator walls: D. W. Dean and Diane Wilkerson. "See? Proof that we were here." But tomorrow morning, the velvet will be wiped clean. He waves at her in the mirror, but she has already turned around, and they are already going down.

EARLY IN THE DAY, the red walls of the elevator are clean, but always, by the end of the day, the smoothness is taken over by finger graffiti. Opposite their initials, on the other wall, there is, pre-dictably, a giant cock and balls traced into the red elegance. When did people start doing that? Drawing dicks everywhere, startling people into acknowledging the presence of their penis or the pres-ence of the trickster who drew it? Rambukwella and Margolotti never had to put up with this, Dean is sure. His mother tilts her head at the giant red velvet dick. It's like she's reading his mind. She says, "There are no penises on the walls in *my* house."

The elevator dings, and the doors slide open to reveal the lobby. The front desk where security works, signing for packages and calling up to tell people about visitors and handling all manner of fuckery, is unmanned, and a young woman with blue hair, her German shepherd in sweeter kicks than Dean, stands with her no-tification of a delivery in hand, waiting for her package. In front of the mailroom, his mother pauses at the display of photographs and notes encased in glass that detail the history of the Red Cars that took Lopez, Rambukwella, and Margolotti all over town, to Long Beach, San Pedro, and San Bernardino. "Look how beautiful it was," she says. "Tasteful and lovely."

"It's still tasteful and lovely," Dean says, and he takes his mother by the elbow, guiding her out of the building. But she doesn't watch where she's going, and so she almost steps into a mound of choco-laty dog shit that someone didn't bother to pick up.

DEAN LIES IN BED, listening to quiet. Monday nights are always the quietest of them all. Not long ago, he and his mother sat out-side in the restaurant below, and they had sparkling wine and pizza served on wooden boards, to underscore the pizza's wood-fired au-thenticity, Dean supposed. Dudes with hair that looked as expen-sive as their women's hair texted during their meals as if always, always, there would be a beautiful woman sitting across from them, and passersby hit up everybody for change, undeterred by the tiny black gate and foliage meant to keep the two Downtowns separate. "Lady," a woman had said, holding out her hand to Dean's mother. "I'm trying to get something to eat." Both Dean and his mother had pretended not to hear her at first, but then they dug in their pockets and purse for change when the woman stood there looking as permanent as a building.

"She reminds me of somebody," Dean said at the time, and then he told his mother the story about when a woman in a wheelchair on the corner of Spring and Seventh had asked him to push her to a bus stop down on eighth. Her arms were tired, arms as old and brown and weathered as a one-hundred-year-old tree branch. Dean was in a hurry, trying to catch the Red Line to Union Station so he could take the Gold Line into Pasadena.

"You just started rolling somebody down the street? Just because they asked you? How long did all *that* take?" His mother cut her pizza with a knife.

"Stop cutting it. It's pizza, Ma," Dean had said. "A half hour at least."

"Where were you *going?*"

And the thing was, nowhere. Nowhere. The woman started out with a place to go, and then, she just kept asking Dean to carry her over here and carry her over there, and he had known that she had come from somewhere else, the South maybe, where people said "carry" instead of "take." She was from far from there, and here is where she would stay.

"That's what happens around here," his mother had said, folding her napkin and placing it over a piece of mushroom pizza with a bite out of it, not cut. "If you're not careful, you can end up wasting your time on a whole lot of nothing."

But now, in the not quite dark, the light from the outside of the building flooding into his room, Dean hears voices, laughter through the walls and a fight between the brother with a Mohawk and his blond girlfriend next door. His mother is wrong. How to explain it, this freaky feeling, pushing that woman around. A feeling like looking over old yearbook photos, from fifty years ago, focusing on a face that came into the world fifty years before you were born and feeling that you had seen the beginning, middle, and end of a person's life. Even his mother had admitted it. Nobody likes to be alone.

He drifts close to sleep but is pulled out again. The building is moving, shuddering with its retrofitted skeleton, moving his bed just slightly. He thinks *Sippy* but says *Lopez*. "Lopez," Dean says. "Elisa," he says, and he recalls that eerie security video he Googled, the last time anyone saw her alive, pushing elevator buttons, lighting them all up, not going up and not going down and, then, stepping out of the elevator into forever. "Sippy," he says again. "Lopez. Elisa. Wilkerson." He says the names over and over, like counting sheep, keeping everyone present like a soothing roll call until he falls, falls, falls asleep.

BECAUSE THAT'S JUST EASIER

Their kid was turning weird. She refused to go outside, unless she was in a car. Overnight, this seemed to be the case. She didn't want to walk. She didn't want to walk out of the front door of their loft, walk down the hall, get in the elevator, walk out of the elevator, and then walk ten paces onto the street and out into the world. No. She'd get to the door and dig in. Screaming and wailing as if she'd lost her mind. The last thing that used to work to get the child out of the house no longer worked. Cupcakes. That was all it used to take. "I bet they have the red velvet today," Frida would say. "Come on, sweetie. You're with me. I'm not going to let anything happen to you." But the last time they did that, just two days ago, a man wearing a blazer with no shirt lunged at them, muttering something about Jesus and the devil. "Devil," he kept saying. "Devil." When he said it, it sounded like "Debil." "Gimme some sugar!" he demanded. He was holding on to the waist of his pants, which had a rope as a belt. His black blazer was so dirty that parts of it glistened in the sunlight. Something like lipstick was smeared on his cheeks, and his long hair stood out at the ends, so that he looked like some deranged scarecrow. He lunged at them with his big hands, near enough to see the length of the nails and the blackness underneath them, and she jerked Dakota's body against her own. But the man was no longer interested in them. He had suddenly changed course, like some prop monster in a carnival ride. He walked on, muttering, and everyone on the street who saw him walked past him, eyes fixed on other things. In front of their building, Dakota begged to be taken back upstairs. "I don't have any sugar!" she wailed, and when Frida tried to calm her down, one of Dakota's bony knees caught her in the chin. Cupcakes were no longer going to cut it.

DOWNTOWN LOS ANGELES WAS a stupid place to raise a child. The move almost spelled the end of their marriage. She was happy in the Valley. They had a house with a yard and a garage. Space and rooms. Jackson had an office all to himself where he kept all his collectibles, his Star Wars memorabilia, his comics. Two shelves full of bobbleheads. Even though it was also his workspace for his photography, Frida liked to go in and stare at his large self-portrait, where he recreated the cover of Isaac Hayes's album *Hot Buttered Soul*. She liked to stare at the smooth brown head, eyes covered in sunglasses, making him a stranger. This is what everyone deserved, rooms full of stuff. And neighborhoods, real neighborhoods with streets that had no sidewalks, streets that had dead ends, cul-de-sacs where children—her child—could run and bike and skate themselves silly. Downtown, even though they could barely afford their rent, gastropubs and sixteen-dollar cocktails and overpriced consignment shops aside, their loft was just two streets up from Skid Row. Every day they witnessed the hard life. There was no getting around the cold hard facts that so many people had nothing. Less than nothing. No getting around the fact that no matter how crazy people were, talking to God, themselves, or the ghost of

Buddy Holly (that was just last week), there would be nobody to help them. The only thing you could do was occasionally reach into a pocket or a purse and thrust money at the person asking for a quarter or a dollar or, sometimes, something to eat. When she gave, she did it without looking too hard or thinking too hard or even smelling too hard, taking tiny breaths until she passed the obstacle. Jackson, though, saw things differently. "I feel like a shut-in," he often said, in his campaign to move. "I want to live in the middle of people, people on top of me and below. On either side." But he spent most of his time in his car, commuting to his Santa Monica office where he was a commercial photographer. He worked long hours to afford their loft, which was at the very top of their building. The skyline stretched out before them, the mountains emerging behind skyscrapers asserting their timelessness and permanence. They were so high up that they rarely heard traffic or much street noise at all, only the strange and mysterious gurglings and clinks of pipes that seemed to be having an ongoing conversation for years.

DAKOTA HAD BEEN FINE, though. Taking the move much better than Frida had, until recently. Frida blamed Jackson for this. Him and his violent comic books. Frida didn't see the value of his collections. Maybe she would if they had been vintage Superman or something, but what Jackson collected was just gross. Guts and gore. They all had big dripping titles like *Horror! Terror! Chills! Weird!* He was big on death these days and had started reading a comic called *Crossed*, about a plague that caused its victims to carry out the most debased and horrible things they could imagine. God. The illustrations. "Are you fucking kidding me?" she'd asked him. She lowered her voice so Dakota wouldn't hear. "Make sure our daughter never, ever sees this shit." Frida, herself, saw those images for days. Dismemberment, blood sprayed all over the place. He also liked *The Walking Dead*. Zombies who beget zombies through contagion. She had made the mistake of being talked into watching the show. "Just one episode. Just one," Jackson had said. "Just watch this one, and I'll never ask you again. If you're not hooked, I'll shut up."

So she did. They put Dakota to bed, opened wine for her and beer for him. Even before anything happened, she was anxious. She didn't want to see anything ugly and started out with her hands covering her eyes. "Nothing's happened yet," Jackson said, pulling her hands down. "And it's fake. Just know that it's all special effects, fake blood, artificial substitutes for the real thing." But she didn't know why the fake thing, meant to look as real as possible, should be any less disturbing. People who watched scary or crazy violent movies with people dying in slow motion, revenge flicks with people getting killed in creative ways, how in the world could they just take it? In this one movie, *I Spit on Your Grave*, which Jackson had made her watch when they were first dating (a concession to his handsomeness), a rapist dies after his victim cuts off his penis in a hot bath. Recalling that, she watched *The Walking Dead,* flinching and covering her eyes the whole time.

Frida was done, just *done*, after she uncovered her eyes long enough to see a zombie in tattered rags take a bite out of someone's face, tendon—or something—stretched out between the zombie's face and the newly dead person, the sound effects making her understand, even if she couldn't see, that the zombie was munching on bone and teeth and everything that was left of that human. "Nope," Frida said, getting up. "Give me points for trying." When she turned around she saw Dakota standing with her dinosaur blanket wrapped around her little body, transfixed on the television. "Monkey, what are you doing up? Don't watch this," Frida said. To Jackson, she said, "Turn it off!" He pointed the remote at the television like a magic wand, erasing all the unpleasantness. But

Dakota didn't seem afraid. She stood, facing the now-black TV, and pointed to it. "Those people look like the people on the street."

"What, Bubs?" Jackson had gone to her and picked her up. "What people?"

"The people," she said. She stuck her thumb in her mouth but kept talking. "The people outside. The ones that look inside the trash. That don't got nice clothes."

"No, Bubs," Jackson had said. "Those people on television are not the same as the people on the street. Those people on the TV were zombies. Zombies are kind of dead. They just walk around," he paused, forgetting, Frida saw, that he was talking to a six-year-old. "They get to be zombies through contagion. They don't see or feel or care about anything except—"

"Are you insane?" she said quietly. "She doesn't need to know or understand anything about—"

"I was just explaining the difference." He crossed his arms, a gesture that she hated. It meant *End of Conversation*. "She should not be comparing homeless people to zombies. Not cool."

"If you weren't a forty-year-old still riding a skateboard, collecting *comics*, you'd know not to talk to a six-year-old about zombies."

"And if you weren't a thirty-five-year-old afraid of her own damn shadow," Jackson said. Because Frida and Jackson rarely, if ever, let Dakota see them fight, Dakota started crying, and saying that she didn't want to be a zombie, like the people outside. "Am I going to get contajeen?"

"I told you," Jackson said. He pushed Dakota's head into the crook between his head and shoulder and pulled on the springy curls of her wild hair. He rocked her back and forth. "I told you she needs to know the difference. She needs to know things."

•

KARA WAS ALWAYS THE passionately cheerful younger sister—
and annoyingly so—with all her activism and enlightenment. She
volunteered at a homeless shelter in Toluca Lake, where they both
were born and raised. She tutored in a literacy project and was a
student at Cal State Northridge. Frida agreed with all of Kara's arguments. Yes, Downtown was being rebuilt. In fact, that was pretty
much a done deal. It was built. Yes, the architecture in the Historic
Core was gorgeous. Yes, it was great for walking, with the Disney
Hall and the Museum of Contemporary Art, The Broad museum
a hop, skip, and a jump away. And the Central Library was world-
class. Six million volumes. Who wouldn't want to raise their child
around music and museums and libraries? But Frida tried to explain. There was living Downtown, as close to skid row as to the
library in *theory*, and then there were the practical aspects of raising
a tiny human being in a city that had the highest homeless popu-
lation in the country, a fact which she had not known, of which
her sister had self-righteously informed her. It wasn't that there
were no homeless people in the Valley or most anywhere else. Everybody sees the man or woman at the off-ramp with his or her
homemade signs, sometimes clever ones about cutting the shit and
just wanting to get a beer. And there was always someone pushing
a cart looking like a little condo on wheels.

"But I think it's good for us to see hard things like that," her sister
had said. "Nobody *likes* to see suffering, but it makes us more empa-
thetic." She drained her coffee, tilting her head back with the cup to
her lips. Frida watched her as she tapped the bottom of the cup to
get the last drop. Her sister and she looked so much alike, and Frida
wanted to grab hold of one of her sister's long blonde dreadlocks
and yank it out. What did *she* know?

You could see and then push those images out of your brain
almost immediately. But the lingering horror, the terror, at seeing
people suffer things that no human being should have to suffer alone,

so visible and invisible at the same time? In, like, herds. That's what they called them on that show that Jackson liked so much.

OF COURSE, JACKSON DID the thing she hated, decided something without her, decided that enough was enough with this not-going-outside business, that Frida was babying their daughter too much, that no kid of his was going to become some weirdo recluse, agoraphobic wackadoo. He'd come home from work and had wanted to enjoy a nice balmy walk around town. It was summer, and the sky was purple, and there was the scent of some sweet flower in the air. The dying sun bounced off the glass of high rises in the distance. "It's a beautiful night," he said, crouching down to Dakota's level. "Bubs, you need to be a big girl about this."

He convinced her to let him carry her out on his shoulders, high above the ground, high above everything. He promised her ice cream. It seemed to Frida that Dakota looked around with big gray eyes so stricken with fear, it was as if she knew the worst thing in the world was about to happen, and her parents, as old as they were, were too stupid to realize it. Nobody could save her. Frida and Jackson stopped when they saw neighbors, a couple from the seventh floor, Jeremy and Frank, owners of a white English bulldog that Dakota had made her own. "Papa," Dakota said. "Let me down. I wanna see Barney." Frida looked at Jackson, and he had that satisfied look on his face, the one she thought was so sexy when they first met, his lips turned up in one corner. One eyebrow raised. And when he let her down, Barney and Dakota stood in the middle of the grown people, as if in a cell constructed of humans.

"You're outside," Jeremy said, stroking Dakota's head and tugging on one of her curls. He pushed his Buddy Holly glasses back up on his nose, and Frida noticed the fine gray hair on his young face, the kind of hair you can only see in the right sunlight. Practically the whole building had heard about the little girl in one of the penthouses who had epic meltdowns whenever she had to leave the building, and Jeremy, Frida supposed, was being some kind of cheerleader. Jackson shook his head and made throat-cutting motions with his hands. *Don't remind her.* And Frank bumped Jeremy with a beefy arm, straining against a blue short-sleeved T-shirt. *What's the matter with you?* his eyes said. Dakota kissed Barney on the lips, and Frida wanted so badly to tell her not to do that, but she was so grateful that Dakota wasn't screaming as though she was getting knifed in the back. She let it go.

"Let's go, Bubbarino," Jackson said, and Dakota hugged Barney as if it would be the very last time she'd see him. She clutched her father's hand, and Frida walked on the other side of her daughter, a reassuring hand on the back of her soft little neck. It was one of those days where the sun was bright and glinty as a knife blade, the breeze gently kissing their faces. Almost at the library, on the corner of Grand and Sixth, there was a man with a handsome face reminiscent of a young Robert De Niro, hair cut military-close, squatting, pants down around his ankles, shitting all over himself. Jackson kept walking, but Frida stopped. Stood stock-still, forgetting Dakota for a minute, until Dakota tugged on Frida's hand and asked, "Mama, is he going to the bathroom?" At that moment, Frida decided to die, just a little. Turn everything off. She did it for Dakota. She didn't want to scare her. She made her eyes dead, so they looked at nothing. She stopped breathing, so she smelled nothing. Her ears heard nothing. She picked up Dakota in this altered state and walked past the man wiping himself with his hand, thinking: *I hope he is crazy, because if he is crazy, he's not here. He's somewhere else.* And everyone around her, so many people, the people going to lunch, to work, for coffee, for drinks, had the same look of death in their eyes, looking straight ahead, everyone catching the same thought as they walked past the man. Keep walking. Just keep walking.

"My pistachio is waiting for me," Jackson called out to them. "Don't you want your strawberry?" Frida walked with Dakota as quickly as she could, past the man, talking the whole time about ice cream flavors.

A block up, in the ice cream shop, Jackson held Dakota up so she could survey all the flavors. She seemed more interested in the ice cream than in the man. While she looked, Dakota shook her hand, the hand that had been held by Frida. "Why are you shaking your hand like that, Bubs?" Jackson took her little hand and massaged it, working on the little dimpled knuckles.

"Mama squeezed my hand too hard," Dakota said.

THEY WERE ALMOST HOME. One more block, and it looked like Dakota would be cured. But there was another man in the distance, lying on the sidewalk. All the people in front of them walked and parted mysteriously, and if you didn't know there was a man on the sidewalk, Frida thought, everyone would seem crazy for suddenly changing course like that, identically, almost at the last minute.

As they got closer to the man, Dakota took Frida's hand and squeezed it. There was a lot of power in that little hand. Her other hand held her ice cream cone, which she was concentrating on fiercely. The ice cream was organic, which Dakota had complained tasted funny at first, although, Frida wondered, how could she possibly tell? But the more Dakota ate it throughout the months, the more she got used to it. They got closer to the man, lying right in the middle of the sidewalk, arms and legs spread as if he had been making snow angels on the hot concrete. When they passed him, Frida looked at her daughter and saw her big gray eyes get small and determined. She licked her ice cream cone. "Is he dead, Mama?"

"No. He's not dead," Frida said, though she didn't know if this was true or not. She told herself that if the man were dead, people wouldn't be walking around him.

"Are you sure he's not dead?" Dakota looked back again.

"If he's dead, there's nothing we can do," Jackson said. He took a napkin and wiped some of the ice cream running down Dakota's hand. "And if he were dead, he wouldn't just be lying in the middle of the sidewalk. So he's probably not. Look. We're almost home."

"But if he's not dead," Dakota said, turning her head again, turning her whole body. "Can't we do something, Papa? If he's not dead, then we should help him."

Jackson stopped. He kneeled in front of his daughter.

"Don't," Frida said, and Jackson held up his hand. *Wait a minute.*

"If he's not dead," Jackson said, "then it's harder."

"Why? Can't we help him and take him somewhere?"

"That's hard, Bubs. Say he goes to the hospital and they fix him, but when he gets out, he doesn't have anywhere to go. Maybe there's something wrong with his brain, and he needs help."

Dakota looked up at Frida. "Can't we take him to where you get the help?"

"Well." Frida knelt down too. "You can't do that for everybody, baby."

"No," Dakota said. She stomped her foot. She did this whenever she got frustrated. It was just her way of saying everybody and everything is so stupid. "I'm talking about just *him*."

"That's hard to do, Honey." Both Frida and Jackson stood up.

"Why?" Dakota said. She pleaded. She really wanted to know. Her little shoulders slumped. They did this whenever she was tired. Jackson picked up Dakota to put her on his shoulders again because he knew the signs for Dakota being tired, but she kicked. "I want to stay *down*." Jackson threw Frida his satisfied look. A look that said, *Hell yeah, my kid wants to walk down the street like a normal person. What'd I tell you?*

When they got inside their building, they let Dakota push the button to her floor, like always, and inside their loft, Jackson raised his hand for a high five, but Frida left him hanging. "Rock star!" Jackson said. He gave Dakota two extra high fives. Frida hugged her daughter long as she could before Dakota pulled away from her, suddenly interested in a coloring book she'd left in the middle of the floor. At dinner, they talked about all the things that Dakota liked. She was turning into a girly girl, which Frida didn't want, but it was happening anyway. They didn't know how it happened, but no matter how many Legos and dinosaurs and trucks they tried to get her to play with, she automatically went to all things glittery and pink and, therefore, barfy in Frida's opinion. So, even though it was summer, she was talking about all the things she wanted for Christmas, mostly Barbie-related.

But in the middle of detailing all the "bestest" things about Barbie's glamour camper, Dakota said, "I think the man on the sidewalk is dead. I think he's dead," she said again and again until finally, Jackson asked why. "Yeah," Frida asked. "Why, honey?"

"I think he's dead," Dakota said, "because that's just easier."

NO BLAMING THE HARVARD BOYS

My mother died telling me what to do. In the hospital, she watched soap operas and reached for me with her big hands as she explained why certain life choices were crucial. When she did this, it made all the tubes stuck into her seem like strings attached to a puppet. She had wanted her best for me: marriage, status, and children. From that list, the only thing she had was the child. We were alone, and so her hands let everybody know the situation. She had cleaned for a living. She cleaned everything with bleach and Comet and Pine-Sol, and she never wore rubber gloves, and so, when I think of my mother, I think of dry, scaly hands and ridged yellow fingernails. I'll give my mother that noble, unappreciated struggle. But what mother would want that for her daughter? I grew up in endless apartment buildings with broken security gates, graffiti tags covered over in paint that never matched. But a nice track home, the occasional night out at Benihana, family dinners where my children were well behaved and the highlight of the evening was someone throwing a shrimp into my mouth, that was what my mother wanted for me. She didn't know anything else.

Instead, I wanted poetry. I wanted beauty and sophistication. Elegance. Style. I wanted parties where one person would mention a poem or a book, and then the other person would have heard of it. That was all. That was everything, if you came from places where that never, ever, happened. I left home to study and to live a different life. These days, sitting at my little desk grading SAT essays, I think of the people at that university and do what everyone does now: search the Internet looking for images. I remember everyone who was in my life a long time ago, and it's something like a television rerun.

I found pictures of this one girl, Jonelle, pictures of a life that seemed really good, for her. In one picture, Jonelle stood with her husband outside one of those houses that looked like a business operation, where doctors doled out prescriptions and burned off moles and cut out basal cells on the spot. It was two stories, her house, a façade of red bricks and bright white columns, plump red roses that were nice accents. All that was missing was the shingle noting the names and services offered. And her husband, he looked like the Harvard man she always wanted. He was tall and looked good in his suit, a proper suit, not one of those loose, juicy-pants, wrinkled double-breasted deals with pinstripes that screamed church. I was glad of that, especially, glad she avoided cliché, at least in that one instance. We ran from cliché in grad school. That was the worst thing anyone could ever say about you, and so the more we tried not to be typical, the more we were, of course. And it looked like Jonelle had gotten the kind of man she wanted, and me, I am alone, the quitter Jonelle said I was, that party night she stopped being Southern and got mean.

Those kinds of parties that we used to have, in Indiana, in the February of winter, when all we wanted to do was drink and find somebody to kiss. Those winters—why do I look back on those moments with longing and resentment, that broken, flickering film that goes flap, flap, flap, forever broken, never to be taped together again? In my mind's eye, the past feels taped together, like a movie, real celluloid documentation. If I got to start over and put the pieces together again, all the people would see that I told you off, Harvard boys. I would go full-on Joan Crawford. Early into the party, before we were all drunk and crunching glass underneath our feet, I wouldn't need liquid courage. I'd straighten my fishnet stockings, smooth the hair on my temple with the palm of my hand, and I would tell you: You can go fuck yourselves. Or, I would tell you, Oh, how we all are so fucked. Cliché. How can you not see this and know this, Harvard boys?

But that was 2000. And Joan Crawford was long dead, reduced to wire hangers despite the miles and miles of celluloid she left behind. Where were my role models? Who were my role models? The same ones you had, Harvard boys, as it turns out.

But I didn't tell you Harvard boys anything, and so that night goes flap, flap, flap whenever I think about it, feeling like a film noir, dark and hard, even in the California sun, me drinking a Moscow Mule and wearing Ray-Ban sunglasses on my lunch break.

You both came in that night, long-awaited celebrities already validated with awards I had never heard of and would never get. Something about a Stegner and something about being proclaimed a genius. One of you was already an editor of a press, barely even thirty and wearing black leather pants and leather shoes with slick soles. The other one of you wore a blazer with a red tank top underneath. What? It was snowing! We wanted to laugh, but then we also understood: You got to wear whatever you wanted to wear, always and forever, like professors who wandered the hallways with no shoes, or with their hair a crazy jumble, or with their hands under the blouse of their prettiest student behind closed doors during office hours. Some people got to do those things. We were not those people, and so the joke was on us. Never, ever would we get to be the kind of professors you rarely see on TV, the real ones, wandering the halls with our hair askew, feeling the cold and sticky linoleum under our pedicured feet. We wouldn't be geniuses who didn't have time for tidy hair or shoes that restricted our creativity. That would make us mad women in the attic who had somehow escaped and needed to be put back in our places.

And I wish you could see this story like a movie, with the villains and the victims spelled out for us all, so much easier, but I'm telling this story like I learned how to tell it in the Midwest, sitting around a table, writing by consensus, my commas and clauses put in place, looking pretty. The work of it, the story, put together in shop. What can I say? It probably still won't add up, but we took ourselves so seriously, sitting around that table. Still, the Harvard boys one-upped us, because they knew: If you were already *worried* about being taken seriously, you were already outside looking through the window with your hands cupped around your eyes, fighting the glare.

THE SCHOLAR AT THE party was Irish, a professor at Trinity, and he *did* look like he had stepped out of a James Joyce novel, the suit, the tie, the crisp cut hair with a rakish flip over his forehead, tinged with gray at the temple. Or it could have been me just making him that, so much better than anyone in the room, after a while. He was the kind of man who seemed too tall for the room. The Harvard boys were disinterested in the party, biding their time as friends of a friend, just passing through. They were taken with the Irishman, since he was from Europe, but this they would deny even under gunpoint. Now I see differently. They cared about African American studies, the Harlem Renaissance, understood the importance of Run DMC, N.W.A., Public Enemy. What else did they need to prove about their alliances, their countenances asked us.

And because it was cold and the wintertime and they were so long awaited after weeks and weeks of nothing to amuse us, my friend Jonelle and I, we believed them. We were one and the same, except she was from the South, with straightened hair and pearls, every day, looking like somebody's mother going to church, a dead ringer for Claire Huxtable. She believed in that old-school solidarity, the us and the them. And she had class, which I, apparently, did not.

I stood, leaning on the stone mantle in our professor's house, the house of a poet from New Mexico who wore '50s dresses with big flowers printed on them, dresses with full hems that swished when she walked. And bright, orangey red cowboy boots. But instead of looking trapped and out of a commercial for Frigidaire, like anyone else in such dresses, she bulged out of them seductively and didn't wipe her cigarette ashes off her hem when she missed the ashtray. Her party invitation had read: HAIRY LOOKING TREES STAND OUT IN LONG ALLEYS OVER A WILD SOLITUDE. SHAVE THEM. THEY ARE NEVER QUITE RIGHT. And the guy that the Harvard Boys had come to visit had said in workshop, "She stole that from Frost and Bukowski and mixed them," as if she'd plagiarized like some desperate freshman. "*Frost and Bukowski*," he'd said, with emphasis, like, *That dumb bitch. Poor thing's aesthetic is a joke.* He said that word, "stole," as if she wasn't a woman who had been writing poetry for thirty years, who knew what she was doing. Instead, she'd pulled an "Oh my God! Is this, like, okay? To put these fragments together? For like, my party invitation?" I should have known not to ask that fool for anything.

But I did anyway. When he came to lean on the mantel, I stared at him. He'd tried to dress like the future he would be delivered into, the life of a professor who looked like an actor playing a professor, tried to look like Joyce or Lawrence but instead looked like a poor man's Faulkner or a young, dark-haired Colonel Sanders. He stood there, adjusting his fried-chicken tie, and I said to him,

"You need to make one of those guys come over here and make out with me." He was getting his PhD and was already ruined, even if it was only his first year. This friend, whatever his name was, looked me up and down. "You're not their type," he said, and it cut me, even though I didn't know how he meant it. I assessed myself. Corduroy miniskirt. Fishnet stockings. Tan suede jacket with fringe all over the place. I supposed I looked like Angela Davis on her way to the strip club—or the rodeo. I didn't look Ivy League, but neither did the Colonel or the genius Harvard boy.

"What type is that? There's two of them. One of them has to be flexible with their types."

"Not *that* flexible," he said, and drummed on his red cup.

But I was drunk by then, or, I should say, drunk already, and so I had convinced myself that all I needed was to learn where to put a fork and a knife, study a map to be able to point out Martha's Vineyard. Or maybe, it wasn't that at all. Maybe it was them who needed the work, too uptight, a whole lot of ivy up their asses.

"They're not that bad," I said.

"What?" he said. "Who even said that?" he said, walking away and leaving me at the mantle. I watched the Colonel walk away, the ass of his seersucker pants sagging. His suit did not fit him as well as he thought it did. To this day, I don't know: On purpose, did he wear seersucker in the wintertime?

Across the room, our professor was holding court, talking to the Irishman. He was sitting in a forest-green chair, and she was at his feet, the length of her dress spread out perfectly, like a fan. Her dark hair curled around one ear, and his legs were crossed, his hitched-up pants leg showing off red, gray, and white argyle, and damn if they didn't look like some beautiful movie, she playing the Grace Kelly to his William Holden. The music in the room didn't quite match, though. Janis Joplin was screeching about being a crybaby. Some people were already kissing in dark corners, and some people were out on the porch smoking. I'd lost track of the Harvard boys and went outside, thinking they'd be smoking cigarettes, looking smart and sophisticated, everybody and everything around me looking smart and sophisticated like any black-and-white photo of the past.

When I stepped outside onto the porch, the screen door creaked behind me and slammed like a moment out of some scary movie, and all around me, ghostly puffs of white smoke floated out of people's mouths and noses. I'd forgotten to close the main door all the way, and one of the Harvard boys said, "Close the door, California." His hair was in an Afro, the medium-sized kind that suggested black nationalism in some vague way. But he wore a tan blazer that matched his skin, a blazer that was less impressive than the navy peacoat that covered it when he first arrived. A few people standing next to him laughed, but I was pleased. "How did you know I was from California?" I smiled, one eyebrow raised. I was feeling bold. I gestured with two fingers for the Harvard boy to give me his cigarette to puff, and he did. He passed it to me. I took a puff and hacked out a cough, grabbing my throat. I didn't smoke. I just thought cigarettes and all the gestures that came with them were sexy. I was trying to get a leg up. Maybe two legs. I tried to give it back to him, and it was moist where I'd puffed on it like an amateur, but he held his hand up. "No, thanks. You can keep it." And somehow that was funny to everybody, too. Jonelle was standing next to him, very close, and they looked good together, she in her pencil skirt and red sweater. That night, she looked like a black Jackie O., a strand of pearls around her neck. Those pearls, she wore them everywhere, all the time, but standing next to the Harvard boy, all of a sudden, she looked like American royalty. She only lacked the pillbox hat sitting atop her sleek, straightened hair.

"No really," I said, hanging on to how the Harvard boy had called me *California*. I dropped the cigarette on the porch, stepped on it, and then picked it up and put in my pocket because I thought leaving butts in someone's yard was for people with no home training. When I shoved both my hands in my pockets, the suede fringe danced. "How did you know?" He looked at me up and down and tilted his head at me, like, *That. That's how I knew.*

The Harvard boy in leather pants, he was the darker one between them, dark like me, his skin looking like a black, velvety canvas against silvery night light. He'd put his coat back on, another dark peacoat, and a black turtleneck covered his neck and brushed against his trimmed beard. Very Black Panther. "But look at *him*," I said, tilting my head at the other Harvard boy, just as he appraised me, his eyes looking large and dark as two eclipsed moons. What were their *names*? But he had just said, "I'm from New York," as if that explained everything.

"He's a genius," some girl said. She was wearing cat eyeglasses and jeans with big cuffs, saddle shoes, too, like some teenybopper from five decades earlier. Everyone at the party had chosen their decades, accidental costumes. "They just told him he's genius." Everyone laughed dry, jealous laughs that reached for irony but fell short. The girl smoothed her black, shiny bangs and drank from her cup. She smoothed her bangs again for something to do.

"Who's *they*?" I asked, and I felt my mouth stretch far and wide to put the emphasis on "they." Everybody shook their heads over me not knowing things I should have known.

"I'm still not over it," the Harvard boy in leather pants said.

"The *money*," someone else said. "Whoever sees that kind of money at one time?" This was coming from the Colonel, who was trying to get outside, negotiating the door, the screen, and his drink. And because he had embarrassed himself with that question and didn't know it, the Harvard boys looked down into their red cups. He weaved his way through to them, since standing next to any of the rest of us was not good enough. Just then the host, the poet, opened her front door and poked her head out from behind the screen door. She smiled at us, showed the gap between her teeth, and the dimples in her cheeks made her look like a kid up to something. We got a blast of warmth from inside, from Sarah Vaughan singing *Whatever Lola wants, Lola gets, and little man, little Lola wants you.* "Not all of you are smoking," she said. "Not all of you standing around in the cold. What are you talking about?" She pointed a finger at us and then let it drop, like she was beginning to count eeny meeny miney mo. She wasn't interested enough to come outside. She stayed half in and half out.

"What else?" This came from a guy named Theodore, who insisted on Theodore, not Ted. That name, I remember, because he had a blue Mohawk, a subtle one, a tasteful nod to Joe Strummer, whose face was on the back of his leather jacket, underscored with THE CLASH in white letters. He said it nice, Theodore. He meant it like it was the only thing *he* wanted to talk about, meant it like he was proud of *poetry* for getting that award, because poetry deserved it. That's why I didn't hold the not calling him Ted against him, or that Mohawk, even though it was 2000 and he was trying too hard.

My professor, being a poet, had heard all about the Harvard boy before he showed up uninvited but welcome. It was a big deal, his award, on its own merits, yes, yes, but also, here it was, right in front of us, in the flesh, the thing Jonelle and I carried around like a backpack overstuffed with books, looking for some place to just put it *down*: young, gifted, and black. And that's a fact. Our professor said, "Congratulations, again. And again," but she, too, meant it generously. She kept all other bromides to herself, the ones about "You must be really happy" or "You deserve it." Instead, she said, "It's fucking cold out here. What are you doing standing around like morons?" She smiled, and it was warm, and she waved us in with a sloppy wave that looked like she was fanning herself. "Come inside," she said. "I have more wine," and when she turned, the screen door slammed on her dress, but she opened it and yanked all that fabric back inside. I was the first to follow her inside, and in the yellow porch light I could see that the screen door had left a dark slash across several of the roses on her dress.

MY PROFESSOR'S HOUSE EMPTIED of all but the most committed and obliged, and so the music seemed louder. Ella Fitzgerald was singing "Mr. Paganini," and her silky, husky voice was sounding crazy and shrill to me, all that scatting, the crazy highs and sudden lows of her singing, I suppose. And my mood had shifted in a way that seemed sudden, but had long been on its way from the moment I'd walked into the house, trying to get drunk as fast as I could. I missed my mother. I had learned since being on the porch that both Harvard boys were taken anyway, the one in the blazer was even engaged to a French girl. That hadn't stopped him from placing his long, delicate hands on Jonelle's waist from time to time, and leaving them there as long as he wanted to. Now, they'd moved to the couch and leaned into each other, faces close, close. Almost. My hope about getting drunk was that you could make out with anyone that you wanted to at parties, and mostly, nobody cared, because everyone else was making out, too. I wasn't jealous of Jonelle and her progress, because I was not done with the other Harvard boy. I was going to get him.

I followed him into the kitchen, where he and the Colonel were standing over the sink, sifting through bottles that were swimming in a watery, icy sludge. The Harvard boy finally pulled out a Rolling Rock. He frowned at the desperation of his choice, and the Colonel stood with a clear plastic cup of red wine. The Harvard boy turned to me. "You want a beer?"

"I hate beer!"

The Colonel winced and then looked at the Harvard boy, a big smile on his face, so happy about making me amusing. Well, I guess I was doing that to myself. I was too loud, which I kind of knew, but I was drunk, so not only did I not care, but I was ramping up to get even louder. I stood next to the Harvard boy, trying to get cozy like Jonelle was doing in the other room. He smelled so good, like Irish Spring or Coast, the kind of plain, out-of-the-box soaps I loved but that made my skin feel like paper. He'd taken off his jacket and pulled up the sleeves of his turtleneck, and so I could see that his skin wasn't dry at all, but looked supple and smooth. I reached out to touch his arm, and he drew back his arm like I'd lit a match to it.

"What!" I said. "I'm not doing anything to you!"

"Stop shouting," the Colonel advised.

"I have a girlfriend," the Harvard boy said. Not mean, no, but tired. He was so tired sounding, I remember.

"Relax!" I touched the Harvard boy again, but that time he didn't pull away.

"Shhh," the Colonel said. "God."

"I'm not trying to marry you," I said, feeling high off his clean smell.

"I just told you about my girlfriend," he said. He peeled my fingers off his wrist.

"She's German," the Colonel informed helpfully.

"Jesus," I said. And I was the one pulling back my arm this time. "How do you find a German?"

"Uh," the Colonel said. "In Germany?"

"I'm not talking to you, smart ass." I tried to glare at him, but my eyes weren't that open to begin with.

"I met her in Germany, last summer," the Harvard boy said.

"Is that what you're going to do with all that money, then?" the Colonel asked. "Travel? God, I'd love to get back to Europe."

"Stop trying to mediate this!" I yelled. "I'm *talking* to him."

But the Harvard boy was ignoring me. He was betting on my going away to pass out in some corner so that he could make his escape, I'm sure. He and the Colonel started talking about all the places they'd been in Europe—Stuttgart, Paris, etc., etc.—and the more they talked, the more I felt jilted, not because I'd never been. Oh, I'd *been*. It was just that my life didn't change the way it seems to change for everyone else when they go. My mother had just died, so my soul did not leave my body, and I didn't come back to the states with the conviction that everything was shabby shit in comparison to Europe. For the last three weeks of my backpacking tour through all those ancient cities, I wrote in my journal, but mostly, all I'd written was *I want to go home I want to go home I want to go home*. I couldn't tell them *that*. This depressed me, proof that I wasn't Harvard-wife material.

"Stop talking about Europe!" I meant to pound on the sink with my closed fist, but I missed and punched the icy water instead, and the water went flying into both their faces. A few pearls of water landed in the Harvard boy's Afro, and he looked adorned and be-jeweled, which made me even more desperate.

Just then, my professor and the Irishman came into the kitchen. "What's this about Europe?" He walked past me, and his arm brushed up against my breast when he reached into the sink, searching for a beer. He looked at the Harvard boy's Rolling Rock. "For godssakes, man," he said, but the Harvard boy shook his head. "That's all there is," he said. "I can't help it."

"Bloody hell," the Irishman said. He picked up a wine bottle and held it above his head, trying to figure out how much was left in it. He picked up the nearest plastic cup, which had somebody's lipstick on it.

"There's got to be a clean cup around here," I said.

"Ah," he said. He poured some wine into the cup and took a sip. He winked at me. "It'll look like I kissed somebody tonight," he said.

"You poor, poor thing," my professor said, without sympathy.

"All the good ones are taken," he said. He sucked his teeth and shook his head.

"Not all of the good ones," I said. I looped my arm around his, but I was still wearing my fringe jacket and didn't like that the heavy suede was getting in the way, so I pulled out my arm and took off my jacket. I placed it on one of the chairs and wrapped my arm around his again.

"I am not responsible," my professor said. "I'm telling you. I'm not."

"Responsible for whom?" the Irishman said. "For what? What do you take me for?"

And my professor said, "Don't make me say it out loud."

But I was happy to be walking out of the kitchen, arm in arm with the Irishman. He was my leading man. My professor put her hand on my shoulder and gave me a look. It wasn't, *Don't do anything that I wouldn't do.* It was more of a look that said, *You're doing exactly what I would have done if I was young and didn't know any better. God help you.*

IN THE LIVING ROOM, Jonelle and the other Harvard boy were making out like I knew they would. She didn't know that about herself, but it was the one thing I knew, even if I didn't know anything else. I'm trying to remember, but I think I was happy for her, exhibiting behavior that would've made her clutch the pearls around her neck if anyone else were doing it. But they were each other's type after all, and even if he had a girlfriend, that didn't spell anything, as the saying goes. Maybe after that night, she would be the girlfriend, the one who snagged the kind of man who rubbed elbows with geniuses. She was a good poet herself, but I didn't give her credit for it at the time because I didn't think that bland, correct-looking people could be poets. That's my fault, getting caught up in the costumes. No blaming it on the Harvard boys.

The Irishman sat in the chair where I first saw him, the deep green one that made him look like a movie star. It was still empty, as though nobody dared to take his seat. He sat down and pulled at his pants just above his knees, to make himself more comfortable, and I swooned at those argyles again, like the idiot I was. He smoothed the sides of his temples, the gray making me want to find a silver cigarette case, open it, and offer one to him. We were all of us ruined by movies, by everything, and this is why nobody dared to sit in the Irishman's seat, and this is why I was wanting so badly to offer him a cigarette from a silver case, just to watch him tap the tip of one on that case, to settle the tobacco and then light it up in a blaze of elegance. He patted his knee. "Come sit with me, won't you?" And the syntax of his request took away any trace of sober common sense I might have had. He put his glass down on the floor. He patted his knee again and sat back in his chair, already making adjustments, making space for me on his lap.

The Harvard boy and his friend the Colonel had come out of the kitchen. They stood against the wall, watching me while the Rolling Stones played and Mick Jagger begged Angie over and over again. I do remember thinking, even if I don't remember so much—like names—that it was such a sad song to be playing during my close-up.

My professor was standing at her mantle, smoking a cigarette, and her dress had accumulated so many stains during the evening, the roses at the hem of her dress were beginning to look like mushrooms. She was talking to Theodore, and in my drunken clarity, I understood that they looked great together, his blue Mohawk and leather jacket, her tattered and stained cocktail dress. So opposite and perfect. Later, after we had all graduated with our degrees, mostly to do anything else but write, people would call her the crazy professor who never had kids and who never got married, who had too many parties and let her students get too drunk. She is my hero. I'll tell you why.

When I sat on the Irishman's lap, I saw her eyes gloss over us but then turn right back to Theodore. Me, I leaned into the Irishman, letting him work a finger into one of the tiny diamond spaces of my fishnets. I only took my eyes away from his to look at the Harvard boy and the Colonel who, to my mind, was judging the Irishman for his taste, and not me. The Colonel called out, "I think you're too heavy for his lap," and the Irishman, whose face was red, but not from embarrassment, said, "It's my lap, mate, and I'm rather comfortable."

The Harvard boy stared at me. He looked down at his shiny leather dress shoes as if looking for an explanation in them. I turned the Irishman's head so that I could kiss him, and I did, stroking the back of his neck like I owned the man. He kissed me back, and as soon as I felt his hand underneath my ass, I was suddenly being pulled up and away by the elbow.

"Ow!" I hollered, even though I wasn't hurt at all. The Harvard boy had me by the elbow. "Cut it out," he said. "He's an old man."

"I'm fifty," the Irishman said, as if that corrected the accusation, but both the Harvard boy and the Colonel nodded, as if to say, "exactly." Even me, I had to nod, the number feeling like a cold splash of sober-up-your-shit-right-now. But when he adjusted his blazer and pulled down his jacket sleeves, his white cuffs peeking out, he still looked every bit the leading man. He grabbed my other elbow and then wrapped his other arm around my waist. The other Harvard boy and Jonelle were standing, since everyone else was, all of a sudden. Jonelle's Harvard boy held up the palms of his hands and told me, "Have some respect for yourself."

Jonelle came to me, leaned into my hair, and hissed some instructions into my ear. She thought she was looking out for me, but to this day, I don't know. "If you fuck this man," she said, "you are just giving up." But to me, if it was something I wanted to do, who were they to tell me not to do it? Who are these people making prescriptions for other people's lives?

"You are not to speak to her this way," the Irishman said, sounding like everybody's father. He hadn't even heard what Jonelle had said. "Do you understand? I'm in charge of this." He pulled me even closer to him, and I could feel the dampness of his shirt underneath his coat. Sweat was beading along his temples. "You're not to talk to her. I'm talking to her."

And then I saw something that I wish I hadn't. When the Irishman said that, everybody listened to him instead of saying, "Fuck you, dude. You're not in charge of shit." I saw it so plain. I saw the Harvard boys looking inside a window, their hands cupped around their eyes, looking through that window at me and the Irishman, window-shopping for something they couldn't afford. Not me. I wasn't worth the change in their pockets. But those words, "I'm in charge of this." That's when they blinked. They believed the Irishman was telling them a cold, hard fact.

But then I heard a loud crash, and something sharp hit the side of my face. I didn't know where the noise was coming from, exactly, so I followed everyone else's faces. It was my professor, who had broken a wine bottle on her mantle—on purpose—like bon voyage-ing a ship. Everybody was watching her with big eyes and then looking down at themselves, brushing off shards of glass they couldn't even see.

"The hell, Carmen," the Irishman said. "Have you gone mad?"

"You're not in charge," she said. "Everybody. Out." But we just stood and stared. My professor made a motion like she was going to crack the bottle again, and that got us collecting coats and moving toward the door.

"Crazy bitch," the Irishman said, once we were all outside the house. We stood, blowing into our hands and stomping our feet. It had gotten really cold. But she had locked the door, turned off the music and most of the lights.

"I'm out of here," the Colonel said. "Let's go," he said to the Harvard boys, but they were already walking ahead of him, treading carefully on the snow-covered stairs. I think I saw the Harvard boy with the leather pants turn his head in my direction for one last look, but then again, why would he have? Jonelle traded numbers with her Harvard boy, but she never heard from him again, of course. And I, well, I went to the Irishman's hotel room, because that was what I wanted to do. It's true that he wasn't so charming when I was sober the next morning, true that he looked every second of his fifty years to my twenty-eight. He was shy, and he kept a towel around his waist like a woman covering her breasts with the bed sheets. But he wasn't the point of that night at all. This is the point: What kind of woman breaks a wine bottle on a mantle? Who wrecks her own house like that, exploding glass all over the place, glass landing into crevices, under spaces nobody will likely ever see ever again? Me, I'm not that kind of woman. At the end of the day, I wasn't raised that way. But I try to be that kind of woman. Still, I'm stuck on half measures. I have broken glass, on accident, and left it on the floor, walking around it for hours until I am ready to clean it. But that's different. That's different from not giving a shit what anybody thinks. Even if you're a genius with lots of money, even if you have class, wearing slick leather shoes in the snow like you don't care what anybody thinks, it turns out you still feel like you have to answer to somebody. I bet you: You've seen too many movies, and you believe what those movies tell you about yourself. You think they're mirrors.

BUILDINGS TALK

W e called him That Fat Bastard Fatty Arbuckle because he was fat and that's all we had. We thought about trying to be above it. I know it's unoriginal and igno- rant to point out the fatness of a guy that huge. But he just looked like every little thing Sussex Properties Trust was doing to us. The rent being raised first 3, then 7, then 10 percent for the last three years. The shady utility company they switched to in the middle of my decade there, with all its hidden "fees," so that the cost of a five-minute shower set us back, like, twenty bucks a pop. I've lived with so many dudes to keep living here. The latest one, Franklin, he didn't even know of a time when stuff that now costs some- thing was free. It's like trying to tell some fifteen-year-old about how back in the day getting your luggage on the plane cost you nothing, because it *shouldn't* have. Like the parking spot that used to be free, that all of sudden cost $150 a month to park my car that only ran some of the time. All this after the romantic years, the years when no one wanted to live in Downtown Los Angeles, where your shoes slipped in blood and spit and urine and vomit, where you yelled at your dog not to sniff the needles in the gutter, because, in fact, you knew exactly where they'd been. And so they courted us, the first in the building. You're pioneers! they said, all chummy and enthused, like they were letting you in on some great real estate deal, when all they were doing was making sure they didn't have any empty apartments. They even gave us duffle bags with the building's logo on it: *Pacific Electric since 1905*. If old building management sniffed the vague scent of us about to jump ship, move to some other building that was trying to fill their apartments, winking and blowing kisses at would-be tenants with other useless but seductive merch, they got all *Please, Sir, please don't go on us*. Begged us to sign a new lease. No rent increase.

But Fatty Arbuckle. He was the most recent in a line of building managers. The others would last a while but kept being shown the door, word was, because they didn't know how to strike the balance between being nice and making money. Me, I hated him from jump because he looked like a dude in costume. And even my roommate Franklin hated him. "He is so not pulling that off," he was always saying, but Franklin was a guy with his own fashion problems that I'll tell you about in a minute. But this new manager: You're asking for resentment and hostility if you're the kind of person who wears a pocket watch and you're on the shy side of thirty. Old-timey rounded collars with thin ties, *bow* ties sometimes. Suspenders on days when he seemed to be daring us to crack behind his back about the fact that a man that fat didn't need suspenders, let alone the belt that wrapped around his body like he was caught in a black Hula-Hoop. He was never going to be one of our favorite people in those kinds of getups, but when he refused to hear out arguments about why, as longtime tenants, we should be shown the courtesy of a lower, hell, *no* rent increase, we went off the rails. Everyday was all things Fatty.

My roommate and I, we sat in the office at a time for which we were made to have an *appointment*, when back in the day you could just wander in and shoot the shit over a too-small Styrofoam cup of hours-old coffee that tasted like lye. They were really doing up the historical aspect of the building, relics they'd found during the excavation and remodel, a few rusted beer cans, somebody's glasses frames. Some ashtrays. When I'd first moved into the building, I'd tripped out over all these old things because it was proof that some guy I didn't even know cracked himself open a beer and enjoyed it and smoked a butt and lived his life. It was like he raised a can for me, the guy way in the future, and said, "Life's a bitch and a laugh, so, aw, fuck it. What are you gonna do?" Look, I know, it's not like they raided some pyramid tombs and pulled up King Tut, but is was something in a city that never feels that old, according to a bunch of dummies who don't know jack. I don't know, my father's father's father was a bricklayer somewhere in England, okay? And in 1905, some dudes laid down some bricks and built a really cool building, not some tan, non-descript stucco crap you can find anywhere around town, but *this*, Pacific Electric Lofts. Lately, though, the beer cans and whatever were just looking like stuff. And the notices that always started with "Dear Valued Resident" tended to leave me butthurt half the time, notifying me of something else that was all of a sudden my problem. The last straw breaking my back was that for safety reasons or something, they had put tiny white piece of tape on all the doors that didn't lead to apartments. The signs, on the *doors*, say THIS IS NOT A DOOR. I just can't. These are the people who rule the world, people who don't know how English works. But Franklin, he thinks it's funny.

In the rental office the walls were covered in grainy sepia-toned wall paper with blown-up images of Pacific Electric Building in the past, before the rooms were lofts, when they were just offices where some guy working toward the next payday punched a time clock. We sat there without being offered our lye coffee, and Fatty was all business. "What can I help you with today?" He leaned back and made a little steeple with his fingers.

We were there because we were done with the 10-percent-increase business. We had to talk this through like reasonable people. Any lunatic would have agreed: That was *so* much more money every month. Were they even for reals?

"So," Franklin started, all reason and politeness. "We've lived here for like, what? Eight years?" He looked at me, and I nodded. Actually, he was my fifth roommate in ten years. Nobody liked to stick around too long. The idea of a loft that wasn't theirs, with rent being raised willy-nilly just *whenever*? Turns out people didn't really like that. Eventually they always ended up telling me in one way or another, *It's been real*, rolling their dollies of hastily broken-down Ikea furniture down the marbled hallway. Franklin was only on his second year, but I'd thought he'd be good ammo against Fatty Arbuckle, since they were representing similar decades, was my thinking. Franklin twirled the corners of his mustache, turned up on the ends in backwards *C*'s. This all of a sudden frustrated me, this fashion problem that I'd mentioned earlier. He put wax on it. I *had* been cool with that, which is embarrassing to admit, until seeing him with Fatty Arbuckle made me feel like I was the freak who wandered in from the future, in a strange costume of black Converse, jeans, and white T-shirt. Maybe I had. It *was* kind of a *Happy Days* look, somebody pointed out to me. Franklin coughed. "I'm sure you know that already," he said to Fatty, "how long we've been here. *He's* been here," he corrected, tilting his head sideways at me and stammering. He was starting out with no conviction. *Dude*, my eyes said. *Focus*. I was going to use his barbershop-quartet ass and then maybe not be all, "Dude, don't move out" when he decided to move on. I had decided that right then. His limp handshake had foretold this moment, my moment of losing faith in the guy. But I don't have that kind of emotional intelligence when I need it. Not when rent is due.

Fatty Arbuckle looked at Franklin and then at me. His kept his eyes doing that side-to-side thing like we were a tennis match, and his smile was spooky as hell, a puppet smile or something. Still as a photograph. It never changed.

"Yeah," I said, trying to recover the fumble. "I think loyalty should count for something. Never missed a payment. I break down all my boxes when I get deliveries. I park straight down in the lot, not at an angle like some idiot that doesn't know how space works. I'm the kind of guy that picks up other people's trash, even. Walking down the hall? I see, like, a cigarette butt or something? I pick it up." Franklin turned to look at me and telepathed the fact that we both had stepped over dog shit in the hallway that some d-bag had left behind walking his dog. But come on. You have to draw a line. "So," I said, "not that you owe me, us, anything, of course. A courtesy. That's all I'm asking. As someone who has been a solid, reliable tenant."

Fatty looped his thumbs under his belt. Sat up straight. Smiled his frozen-in-time smile. "I understand you have been a good tenant. Sussex Properties respects your tenancy. But we cannot make distinctions between tenants. Those who have lived here for a long time and those who are new."

"Old management did," I said, and Franklin nodded, even though he was just passing through and didn't know shit about old management.

"That was then, and this is now," Fatty said. He shrugged, but his face still had that mask smile. I studied the rolls of his neck, wanting to work my way into them, to the bony, chokeable part. "Look," he said, holding his palms up. "This is a corporation. What-ever the market dictates, that is what we do. As long as the price of rents go up, so, too, will the rents at Sussex Properties Trust." He delivered this brutal honesty with a dimpled smile, and I real-ized that he didn't look like Fatty Arbuckle at all, but Hardy from Laurel and Hardy. We'd gotten our fat guys mixed up from the very beginning.

"So, that's it?" I looked at Franklin, but his eyes said, *I got nothin*.

"You're welcome to consider other rental opportunities," Fatty said.

"You mean, like, move?"

"I mean that you may find other, more suitable arrangements for your situation," he said. His eyes were brown and shiny and full of comedy. "Would you like a cup of coffee?" He gestured toward the coffee machine, cups, and sugar across the room.

I stood up, and Franklin did, too, late, turning to look at me while he did it, like he'd forgotten the steps to a dance routine. "I'll let you know what we decide," I said, trying to sound tough and savvy, as if he was in danger of losing me, as if he needed me, as if I wasn't just a part of a long line of people who had lived lives in apartments, gotten screwed over by some landlord or another, and moved on, part of a long line of people and their ghosts, in a building that was built before movies had sound.

I LOOKED ALL THIS stuff up. I may be cashing this week's check on Friday and broke by Monday, driving a forklift at FedEx, a waiter before that, McDonald's and Burger King when I was kid and didn't know any better, but now I know how things work. If a building is refurbished in L.A. after 1990, even if the building is old as hell, like my building, it doesn't count for rent control. So Fatty or Hardy or whatever his name was had some legs to stand on with his smarmy ultimatums. If I didn't like it, I was "free" to leave because now there were plenty of what looked mostly like twenty-five-year-old kids with mysterious jobs that paid them in buckets of cash so that they could afford three-thousand-dollar-a-month rent. Everybody was *stylist* or *blogger* or some crap. *Downtown*. Me, I was forty. And yes, I'd had it good for most of my years in the building, and, after all, I was one of those kids ten years ago, moving in and

pushing out people who lived Downtown before anything was refurbished, when they paid three hundred dollars a month for rooms
and walked down the hallway to take a dump and brush their teeth.
I had no business complaining about being chased out. Still. I'm
asking. Where are people supposed to go? Where *do* they go? Does
it really come down, always, to the cold, cold, hard, hard, cash? I
know. Where have I *been*? But I'm telling you. Down in the lobby
they had this old-timey directory with folk's names that used to live
and work in the building. Crazy names with eight vowels in a row
followed by ten consonants. *Long*-ass names. That directory? That's
some scary stuff right there. Who wants to get off the elevator and
look at the names of ghosts every day? My point is this: People's
time in places has got to count for something. You don't just yank
the lye-tasting coffee out of a guy's hand after ten years. I blamed
Fatty Hardy for his Sussex Properties corporate, humanity-killing
policies. All this was his fault with that ventriloquist dummy smile
of his. That was what I thought at the time, and still do, really, but
mainly I just needed somebody to pay for the injustice of some
people being rich as hell and other people being forty years old
with rotating roommates. I started watching the guy more closely,
revenge in my heart. Nothing crazy like a mysterious pratfall down
a flight of stairs or busting his noggin on a slapstick banana peel in
one of our ancient, tiled hallways. Just a little humiliation to take
him down a peg. Let him have the feeling of staring at a wall with
suspenders and dimples.

I tried to get Franklin on the case, too, but the disassem-
bled-Ikea-furniture writing was on the wall. He wasn't going to be
my roommate for much longer. He was already making noise about
how the extra 10 percent was going to be steep, and he didn't
know, so on and so forth. "I dunno know, man. Kinda steep. I can
check out Culver City for that price. It's supposed to be pretty chill
over there."

When I watched Fatty Hardy, as it turned out, I learned a thing or two, for real. Dude was ruthless. Turns out, we got off light in his office. That was him being warm and hospitable. He was tearing the work crew new ones on the regular, but only when he thought he wasn't being watched. When he didn't think eyes were on him, he played the warden. "Javier. Get this mop and broom out of the way. We're always *showing*, you know that." Or "Hector. Don't you ever leave the security desk for longer than five minutes. We need someone present *at all times*." One time he caught me looking at him. He was yelling at Janet. Nice. Always talked about how hot it was in the lobby, didn't I think? She always wiped down the fake red velvet in the elevators before they replaced the red velvet with some kind of material you couldn't write or draw on. People used to write "fuck you" with their fingers and drew uninspired dicks that were majestically lit by the halogen lights in the ceiling of the elevator. One day she forgot to use the lemony-smelling stuff to cover up the funky smell of dogs too big to be living in apartments in the first place.

"If I get in another elevator," he said, pointing a finger in her face, "and it don't smell like lemon? We're going to have a problem."

"Yes, sir," Janet said, nodding, and some braids fell out of her scarf and onto her face. Hot. She was hot. Not a part of the story. I'm just saying. Right when I stopped looking at Janet, though, was when I saw Fatty Hardy see *me*. Up popped the puppet smile. But before that, there was a moment. Maybe he saw what he looked like through my eyes: a guy way too big to be looming over and pointing a finger at a woman who happened to be not his color. Yeah. It looked bad. My eyes agreed with his eyes. But then the moment was gone, and we were back to the dimples. He gave me a nod and strolled back to his office. Another time, in the lobby, I watch him bend over to pick up a piece of something on the floor, and when he bent over, his ass looking like a pinstriped mattress,

I was hoping so bad that his pants would split straight down the middle with the loud sound of ripping sheets, laugh track in my head. But no luck. When he stood up and turned around, what he saw was a dude staring at his ass. His eyes got small, trying to figure out my motives, but this time he didn't even bother with the nice act. He nodded, his lips pinched together, and gave me a look that said, *Why should I be nice to you, you goddamn pervert?*

STILL, I GOT WHAT I thought I wanted. I saw Fatty Hardy go down.

There's this big conference room in the lobby, with glass walls so you can see in. Whoever's in there working or whatever. It's supposed to be for anybody in the building, but I never see anyone but the old guys who own the building in there. About four months after Franklin and I dropped our pants, bent over, and got charged another 10 percent, Fatty Hardy was sitting in the room with three guys with white hair, striped oxford shirts. I was sitting in one of the truly stupid, overlarge silver chairs that were supposed to be all about deco elegance or something, pretending to go through my mail. Franklin buzzed himself into the lobby just then and sat on the arm of my chair.

"What are you doing? You never sit down here." His eyes followed mine. "What's that all about?" He tilted his chin toward the conference room. There was lots of hands waving, nods, staring into space, notes being taken. "I'm trying to see," I said. I was talking out the side of my mouth, trying not to move my lips.

"Are you purposely talking like that? What are you, some spy now? Nobody cares," he said. "They can't even hear us." He looked back at the room. "Jesus. Look at the sweat on Arbuckle. It's really coming down."

"Hardy," I said.

And then, the conference-room door opened and the old guys came out, all of them wearing pleated khakis and loafers. I don't know what got into me, but right then, I would have taken Fatty Hardy's suspenders and rounded collars over any one of those guys' bread-colored pants and loud Easter-looking shirts. Timeless. One of them patted Fatty Hardy on the back. He shook his hand and said the worst words in the world that one human can say to another human. He said, "Good luck."

BUILDINGS TALK. THAT'S THE cool thing about them in case you don't live in an apartment. It's true: Maybe I don't really know anybody in a building of, what? Three hundred lofts or something? But how do I know all the stuff I know? That's what I'm talking about. The building's got a big mouth. That's how I know that Fatty Hardy lost his job, and that's how I know he lost it by trying too hard to hold on to it. The dudes in the khakis weren't fucking around. They wanted mo money, mo money, mo money. They made Fatty Hardy the enforcer, but that was his doom. So many people said, "What do I need to pay another two hundred dollars a month for? I'm out." I saw it coming, myself. The big turnover. From my apartment window, I could see into the windows of so many empty apartments across the way, and those windows looked like eyes staring right back at me, like, "What are you looking at? You're next."

Maybe a week later, Franklin and I went downstairs to the bar underneath the building, Cole's. It's the oldest bar in L.A., built in 1908. They sell French Dip sandwiches and cocktails that are tasty, and there's a speakeasy space in the back with even better cock-tails, people say. But me, I'm not a mixology type of guy. I'm just a straight-whiskey-in-a-glass, no-ice type of guy. I just like places with liquor. But I'll tell you the thing I like best about the place downstairs: It's the first place in L.A. that had a check-cashing service, way back in the day. I like the idea. You get your check cashed, get yourself a sandwich and a nice pop of something not fancy but strong, and you're good to go.

When Franklin and I got to Cole's, we saw right away, bellied up to the bar, there was Fatty Hardy. There were exactly two seats left, of course, right next to him, and so Franklin pretended that he had to tie his shoes when we were walking up to the bar, I guess so I'd have to sit next to him. Jackass. That made me get to him first, but then I took the seat next to the seat *next* to Fatty Hardy, because Franklin's no chess player. He couldn't see the move after his. "Jerk," he said as he sat down.

"What?" Fatty Hardy halfway turned to Franklin and took a sip of something brown.

"Oh. No," Franklin said. "Him. I was talking to him." He pointed his thumb my way.

Fatty leaned over. When he saw it was me, he held his glass up in a toast. I didn't know what *that* meant. It gave me the creeps. He and I? We were not cool. We were definitely not *down*. He was *not* my peeps. Thanks to him, around the same time the next year, I'd have another roommate, this one with a 1980s Mohawk and those fucked-up plugs in his ears that stretched them to shit.

But a funny thing happens when you drink with somebody. You get to be somebody's history, the memory of a stranger. That night we had some laughs, sure, but also, I remember this: We were steady getting drunk, but I was getting sad. Fatty Hardy kept saying, "You're all right, the two of yous" and "That looks all right, that moustache" to Franklin. Fatty Hardy kept putting his sentences out of order and sounding weird like somebody's grandfather from the old country. I started missing him already, and that was good, I guess, because I never saw the guy again. And my new roommate, I can't say to him and have him understand, no matter how big his drooping ears are. I can't say, "Member that one manager? Fatty Hardy? That belt he used to wear? *Damn*."

That night was a good night. The back bar is old, dark and oaky looking, soft lights and the names of guys from years and years ago who drank enough to have their names up there from way back when to now. The music was good. First Bowie then Aretha, then Zeppelin. In the mirror of the back bar, I could see the framed black-and-white photos on the wall behind us, people who were history looking back at us in the mirror. One of them looked like Marilyn Monroe.

"Marilyn Monroe!" I turned around and pointed. There was a guy next to me with a huge Afro. "Naw, Dude. That's some other lady that just look like her." He pointed at me. "James Dean!" "No, no, no," his friend said. He pointed at me and covered his mouth with his fist. "Oh shit. You know who that motherfucker look like? What's that dude on *Happy Days*?"

"Screw you guys," I said. I was so faded. Franklin was working on some girl with a ring in her nose, I remember that, and by then Fatty Hardy was gone. Vanished. I said it again. I said, "Screw you guys!"

"Man," the guy next to me said. He pulled on my T-shirt. "Sit your drunk ass down."

"No," I said. "No! My name is Marty Allen Jones, and I been living here for ten years, and I'm going to live here for ten more, maybe even forever, and I'm home and ain't going nowhere!"

ART IS ALWAYS AND EVERYWHERE
THE SECRET CONFESSION

This is a secret, what he's about to do. He has told no one about this. He doesn't tell anybody, *can't* tell anybody, because he takes himself seriously and they'll give him so much shit. But it's his therapy, this thing he does. It truly makes him feel better—and can something really be lame if it actually does the world good? By "the world," of course, he means himself, and, by extension, the world. He's not narcissistic, as his friends have accused him of being, but simply *aware*. How he sees it—and nobody can really call bullshit on this—is that a happy person, or at least a person who is feeling all right in his skin for at least a decent amount of time on any given day, generally is not compelled to be a bad citizen and put crap vibes out into the world. A happy person behaves himself. And so he does this thing to make himself happy.

He's not perpetually bummed. That's not the situation. The situation is that often he's bored. He needs contrasts. He gets sick of himself. He's exhausted and exhausting. For a thirty-year-old, this disposition can feel like a never-ending marathon. And he knows that boredom is one of those so-called first-world problems—a phrase that is, he likes to point out, un-PC. You're trying to call

somebody out on his privilege while ascribing a hierarchical sche-
matic and thereby judging which nations are first, second, and
third? By whose standards? But he can't get started on all that.
Not right now. He's got his therapy to get to. Has to get going to
his secret place, the place about which all his friends, who call him
Marx, as in Karl, would give him shit if they knew that *this* was
where he went for peace of mind. Because he's the guy who ruins
everybody's fun. Right when you're about to take a bite of your delicious slice of pizza, he'll ask you: How can you even eat food from
there? They give money to blah, blah, and whosits. I hope denying
people basic rights tastes delicious!

(Or, How can you even wear those jeans? I hope child labor is
sexy to you. The kids who make those? They get, like, negative five
cents for working eighty hours a day.)

He can be the worst. He knows this, and that's why he makes the
drive that he does, all the way from Downtown to the Westside. He
pulls out of his parking lot on Main Street and drifts past the historic mortar-and-brick buildings that usually give him comfort. He
makes the left on Temple and stays on Temple, driving out beyond
Downtown and through Silver Lake, until Temple turns into Beverly, taking him through neighborhoods that turn from Korean to
Salvadoran to Jewish. Beverly. Beverly, of course. The Hills not so
far away. The street brings him closer to everything he perpetually critiques about capitalism and the bourgeoisie, everything that
truly brings out the buzzkiller in him, but when he pulls into the
Grove, winding round and round up and up into the parking lot, he
gets that calm-yet-elated feeling. Like taking medicine and feeling
it working on you. No more suffering. Karl Marx feeling good and
buzzed.

The Grove. He knows that when people think of Los Angeles,
this is the city they see, the little city of this shopping center. Not
the beaux arts buildings of Downtown, the kind of stuff you can

scope out in Chicago or New York. Beautiful, yes, that architecture, kingly griffins staring out at you from twelfth-story ledges, but not as shiny and new and glistening, as bathed in the bright amber sun of California, as the Grove. It's like Disneyland, he's said many times, rolling his eyes just thinking about the garish shops and, especially, the enormous tree erected every Christmas, several stories high, guarded by psychotic-looking nutcrackers baring their painted teeth at him.

But he always comes back. Gliding down the elevator, he can start to hear what he's there for. Frank Sinatra is singing about the summer wind that came blowing in. He walks toward the center of the mall, restaurants on either side of him, the pathway opening up to shops, the movie theater, the trolley that travels its short distance while the conductor clangs the bell. The fountain, though— God, good God, it's so embarrassing that he loves this fountain so much. "La fuente que baila," he heard a mother say to her daughter. A fountain with choreographed dance moves that gyrates to Frank Sinatra and Donna Summer. He arrives in time to see perfectly orchestrated jets of water shoot up into the sky and then entwine, mist lightly spraying his sunglasses, the soft thunder of crashing water and Frank's smooth-as-hell croon giving his nerves a therapeutic massage.

He will never tell anyone.

He'll linger here for another song or two, and later, still hidden behind his sunglasses, he will sit outside one of the restaurants and have a martini with three olives, beads of condensation forming on his glass. He'll look for the celebrities he swears he could not care less about, and he'll get the thrill of recognizing that guy. (You *know*. The guy. The one who was on that *show*.) He'll watch impossible women pass by, looking ugly beautiful the way models do. He'll walk down the same road that the trolley takes, go into the maze of the Farmers' Market, feeling the decades swell up around him because he can smell those eighty years in the breeze. He'll get some fruit, papaya maybe, that's been sitting on ice and hold it, feeling the cold before he hands it over to be bagged. And then he'll get an ice cream cone and eat it, slowly, on the way to his car.

THE LIBERACE MUSEUM

"You're spoiled," he says, when they arrive at their motel. He juggles their baggage the best he can. It's not heavy, he says, but she knows he's lying, because he's just a bit stooped from his weight, tilted. His lanky frame, usually straight as a beam, has turned into a leaning tower. "Everything I hand to you, just because you ask. I wish I were in your shoes. I'd be on easy street, I tell you what," he says. *I tell you what*, she thinks, and smiles, tickled by his Southern talk. "I don't have a prayer," he says, leveling his brown eyes at her. She stares at him, his wide eyes connecting the three freckles across the bridge of his nose. "I'm a dying breed," he says. "A man who calls the shots." At the desk, he puts down the bags, strokes her cheek, and leans in to kiss her.

"You mean a man who *thinks* he calls the shots."

"I said *dying*, not *dead*. You are spoiled, but I'm still the ask*ee*, not the ask*er*."

"Well make up your mind," she says, squeezing his free hand while his other hand takes a pen from his pocket to sign for the hotel room. "Either I have the edge, or I don't. Either the world is, and will always be, yours for the taking, or not."

Distracted, he circles the pen around the page, trying to figure out where to sign his name. Then he does sign, in elegant, ornate cursive that looks as though it could have been written with a quill pen: *Heath Bolinger.* "What are you *talking* about?" he asks, putting a period at the end of his name for emphasis.

Actually, Charlotte isn't sure. She thinks the shot-calling in their relationship is more of a tit-for-tat sort of thing. She labors for the things she wants. Negotiates.   Only suckers get nothing for something, so she'd acted up and carried on, in her way, until he agreed to visit the one place in Vegas she really wanted to see. She *wheedled*, which was usually beneath her, dirty words in his ear at inappropriate times, not beneath her. Sly gropes under the table at truck stop diners, in between BLTs and pecan logs. And finally, actual tit. Just a little bit, just a flash as she came out of the restroom at a Stuckey's. He had asked Charlotte what had gotten into her, pretends that his Southern sensibilities are compromised every time, but Charlotte knows better. She can see the truth in his eyes. She can always see it in his eyes if she pays careful attention, looks straight into them. "Okay, silly," he'd said, his thin lips pecking her full ones when he finally gave in to her request. "Give you an inch, you take a mile. First Vegas, just a quick stop, and now some shrine to a cheesy homosexual."

She nodded vigorously. "Yes, yes, yes."

He is in a hurry though, traveling cross-country so he can help her get settled in Los Angeles, in their loft Downtown, and then get back to New York, civilization, to pack up everything, his whole life, for her, so she can teach history to college students. He'll be taking a job for the city, planning the urban landscape of Los Angeles, as if there is anything left to plan. "Your destiny is all tapped out, sweetie," she told him while they where packing boxes. "The West has been won."

"Silly woman, there is *always* something to be won," he'd said, grabbing her and manhandling her like Rhett did Scarlett. Two of his favorite historical figures, still, unironically, even after Charlotte explained why this was problematic. They'd stumbled and fallen laughing into the boxes they'd just assembled. They'd bent them some, but the boxes all remained square and solid.

Now, they are in Oklahoma, and he likes to do most of the driving. "We've got to speed through Oklahoma," he says, rushing past the ice machine. "Dang it," he says, banging his knee against one of the suitcases. He'd requested a bellboy, someone to pass the bags off to, but the lethargic woman at the desk pulled at one of her dream-catcher earrings and reminded them both, with, it seemed to Charlotte, a tone tinged with scorn, that this was a *motel*. "It's killing me, this place. Full of nothing. Flat, flat, and more flat," Heath says, still shifting bags, readjusting his grip. "And there's a lot of road ahead of us, Charlotte. A lot of land for me to conquer," he says, winking.

But Charlotte thinks Oklahoma is beautiful American land, full of possibilities. She wants to slow down and has planned a leisurely trip, asking the woman at the AAA for a TripTik that would give them a guaranteed gorgeous view of America. "Heath," she says, bursting into their shabby room that smells of disinfectant. "Baby. How many times are we going to get to do this, see America? Purple mountains majesty!"

"I'm whipped," Heath says, pulling Charlotte onto his lap. Their Super 8 bed wobbles as if it is one pin away from collapsing. "You get the whole shebang, sweetheart. Like our hinds are on fire, we're out of this place tomorrow. And we'll stop in Vegas. He puts his hand underneath her blouse and finds her breast, which he massages. She wears her hair in braids, and he runs his pale fingers through them from root to tip and kisses her on the nose, as if sealing a deal without a handshake, but with a handful of something else. "Just explain to me what the Liberace Museum has to do with America."

"*Honey*," she says, kissing his chin. "That's so obvious. Excess, excess, excess. Besides," she adds. "It'll be hilarious."

"Hilarious."

"Don't you think? All that glitter, all that conspicuous consumption, jewels on top of jewels on top of jewels? And sequined hot pants."

CHARLOTTE KNOWS THAT HEATH and hilarious don't go to-gether—not the way she thinks they should. She loves him, but their humors aren't a match. He's not a silly man. Puns are a no-go. He's willing to take irony only so far, whereas Charlotte thinks irony is essential to surviving life, like water, like air. He's a serious man. A smart man. That, she loves. A PhD in urban planning. He's from Mississippi too, which is charming. She was taken with him her first year of grad school, from the very moment he tapped her on the shoulder and asked, "Ma'am, could you direct me to the li-berry?" When she turned, she expected to see an aw-shucks hick with his hat in his hands. Instead she saw a tall, looming man with a quiet composure, looking something like that actor Jimmy Stewart, who had, it was clear from his predatory eyes, already as-sessed her and found her to his liking. And this was what Charlotte liked about Heath, aside from his smarts and kindness: that rawness in his eyes, his plain and honest thoughts just beneath that placid surface of Southern hospitality. They'd gone out of their way, to Bir-mingham, Alabama, to visit the Civil Rights Institute—Charlotte had insisted—but back on course and headed toward Los Angeles, they'd stopped in Jackson, Mississippi, so Charlotte could meet Heath's parents. When Charlotte first saw the house, something straight out of the movies, she wanted to nudge Heath but thought better of it, what with his lack of irony and all. But in the end, she did anyway. When his parents were out of earshot, she poked at him and gestured at the endless porch and glistening white rocking chairs, at the grand white house—with *columns*—and said, "My, my, my. All that's missing is the darkies." And Heath should have said, "Nuh-uh, you're here, aren't you?" It would have been a relief, hilarious in that ironic, we-have-so-much-distance-from-the-past-so-we-can-joke kind of way, because it would have been true, only the circumstances under which all of them were brought together, standing in the sitting room of that big house, looking like something straight out of a slave narrative, would have been different. But Heath frowned. He didn't think it was funny. "People use this house all the time," he said. He ran his large hand up and down the creamy white columns admiringly. "They get married here, hold gatherings here. They want to be close to history."

"Do they?" Charlotte placed her hand on top of his while he caressed the column.

"Of course they do," Heath said. "What a question."

Later, at dinner, Charlotte half expected to be served by hired help, but Heath's mother cooked and served, was polite, a tiny raven-haired woman with delicate features and an apron wrapped around her simple turquoise dress. His father was kind and handsome. A bit of a flirt. Short. Shorter than Charlotte, so short that he almost looked like a little person, and Charlotte wondered where Heath's height came from, being from such tiny people. She chocked it up to the mysteries of southern DNA. Heath Senior's accent was thicker than she'd ever heard; she could hardly understand him at times. "You sound much more Southern than Heath does," Charlotte said, perhaps because of the wine. For a moment she was afraid she'd insulted him. But he laughed and pulled her close as they stood outside on their expansive porch. A veranda,

Charlotte supposed. Not a porch at all. Heath Senior wrapped his stubby but somehow heavy arm around her and grinned at his son. "I've been all over the world just like Heath, here. And no matter where I go, I know my place. No need for me to forget about my raising with none of that fancy talk. Ain't that right, son?

"See?" Heath had said, after Heath Senior left them alone. He enveloped her, and they stood alone on the veranda, facing vast woods. Charlotte looked into the thick forest. "I told you," he said. "You were anxious for nothing. They don't even think about race."

That night, Heath held her tightly, and Charlotte stared out into the dark woods that, as his father told them proudly at dinner, his family had owned for 150 years. She thought about how long ago a hundred years was, and thought about who was free to own what. She couldn't help but wonder. It was an obvious connection to make. Automatic. But Mr. Bolinger didn't talk about that at dinner, and it wasn't the kind of conversation to have when you were first meeting someone's parents—when you were black and first meeting someone's white parents. She was in love with Heath and would not allow herself to make a mistake, not allow room for misunderstandings, botched first impressions. She spoke impeccably, organizing her sentences before she spoke them, blunting the end of each word with precise pronunciation. She dressed impeccably, sweeping her braids into a bun so that the Bolingers wouldn't have to puzzle over her hair. Impeccably, without uncertainty or hesitation, she executed every dictum of manners expected, she imagined, by the Bolingers, of Southerners, or white Southerners, of someone such as herself, who could fold into any fabric, who would never call attention to the fact that any work was being done at all. It was automatic, yet exhausting, like a dancer's hundredth performance in a Vegas show.

"You were great, honey," Heath said. "You always make everyone feel so comfortable."

Charlotte had watched fireflies flicker in the darkness and be-tween the trees like small, distant torches. The land that the Bolingers owned seemed to go on and on into that darkness. She wondered if the slave quarters used to be out there, among the fire-flies. *One hundred and fifty years ago*, she thought. *And here I am, free as a bird*. "It's so dark out here, Heath," she said. "Let's go inside."

"You're the boss," he said. And then, when she flinched as he grabbed her wrist to lead her into the house, he laughed. "It's your choice. Inside or out?"

Charlotte looked down at his arm resting on hers, noticed his red, gleaming hairs standing erect and prickly against his creamy skin. She hesitated and stared out at the little torches.

"Better come inside with me, where it's nice and comfortable. I hear those woods are full of ghosts," he said in his best Dracula voice, phlegmy and vaguely European. He laughed at Charlotte's frown. "What? You're so funny sometimes."

In Vegas, Heath complains that things have gone from bad to worse. Through the haze, from their fourteenth-story room at the Monte Carlo on the strip, they can see the Eiffel Tower. "The things I do for you," Heath calls out to Charlotte in the bathroom. "Okla-homa's looking real good to me right now." He shields his eyes as he surveys the lavender skyline. "And look at *that*. A *rollercoaster*. On top of a *hotel*. In the middle of the *city*."

"Wait until you see the pyramid," Charlotte shouts. "You'll really fall apart then."

"This place breaks my heart."

But Charlotte thinks Vegas is exhilarating, a breath of fresh air, the seductive glamour of darkness always turning into the glaring truth of daylight. New hope and new luck every single day.

She is organizing her toiletries, because she always thinks tidying makes it easier for whoever is cleaning the room to do their job.

She and Heath have splashed water spots and toothpaste all over the sink and mirror, so she takes a piece of tissue and wipes all that down too. She always does this. She can't help herself. But Heath doesn't notice anymore, the work she does so that they're always neat, easier. He only notices when life is not easy and neat. Before turning off the light, she looks at herself one more time in the mirror to make sure there is nothing unexpected on her face. "You're so uptight," she calls out. "This is Vegas, not the end of the world. It's fun; let's have some fun."

Heath turns to face her as she closes the bathroom door behind her. He's gnawing on leftover chicken brought in from the car. "I'm starving. Let's go get some shrimp cocktails or whatever people eat around here." He tears one more bite off the chicken leg and tries to toss the bone in the trash bin. He misses, grabs his wallet from the TV stand. "Ready?"

Charlotte looks at the bone on the floor and then at Heath.

"What? The minute we're gone, one of the cleaning people will come in."

"I know."

Heath shrugs and leaves his trash on the floor. "This isn't a Super 8. Leave things sometimes. It won't kill you to leave things as they are. In five minutes, the bone will be gone, everything will be all cleaned up, and you won't even know it was there."

Charlotte picks up her bag. She walks over to the trash bin, pulls a tissue from her bag, and picks up the bone with it. The bone makes a hollow *plunk* sound when it hits the bottom of the can.

"Happy now?" Heath asks, not waiting for her answer. At first he thought her cleaning habits were cute; she was caring and conscientious. Later, after witnessing the ninth or so hotel pre-cleanup, he accused her of having a neurosis: newly middle-class guilt, the apologist for The People. No, it wasn't that, she told him, and it isn't, not exactly.

She's just been taught to be responsible for the mess she makes. She just doesn't want anybody thinking she's a slob who leaves toothpaste splattered all over her bathroom mirror. Something so simple, always part of a ping-pong consideration. That's neurosis for you. They. They always are dirty, tearing up and running down a place. A group of them is nothing but trouble. We. We have to make sure we're never dirty, never tearing up and running down a place. This is the lesson drummed into her head by her mother, who is a teacher, and her father, a postman, her whole life.

EVERY DAY FOR YEARS and decades, the Williamses followed their regime: Mrs. Williams drove the same route to the same elementary school for thirty years, and Mr. Williams walked the same route for more than forty years. And every dime they saved went to Columbia University, the alma mater of their only child.

"You will do well," her mother said. "More than well," her father said. "You don't ever want to give nobody an excuse to deny you from nothing."

The first time Charlotte was denied, she came home crying because she wasn't chosen classroom leader in her fifth-grade gifted class. Charlotte's mother told her to dry up. "You'll be crying for the rest of your life if you get your feelings hurt every time white folks don't give you something," her mother said. She rubbed Charlotte's tear from her face roughly, as if she were rubbing off a stain.

"It's not cause they white!" Charlotte wailed. "They like me."

"They *are*," her mother said. "Not 'they.' We use proper pronouns, *with* verbs." She studied her daughter and crossed her arms. "*Because*, not *cause*. And what are you wearing? You got no business wearing that loud outfit if you planned on getting elected to something."

Charlotte was wearing her favorite purple paisley blouse with pink tights. Nobody else dressed up church-special that day. It wasn't supposed to be a big deal, the whole choosing-the-leader part. She looked down at herself and pulled at her tights. "This is all right. Everybody else wore what they wanted."

"Well, you are not like them," her mother said, "going to school looking just all right. And you don't want to be wondering, next time, in a room full of white people making decisions about you, you don't ever want to be wondering: What if I had dressed better than all right? What if I hadn't worn something all loud, calling the wrong kind of attention to myself? What if I had looked one more time in the mirror? They are always going to have something to say about how we do things."

"They *are not* making decisions about *me*," Charlotte said. "It's just about who's going to lead the class. They're thinking about everybody the same."

"Right," her mother said. She pursed her lips. "What did you do when you found out you didn't get what you wanted?"

"Nothin."

"*Nothing*." Charlotte's mother crossed her arms and considered her daughter. "I guess that's about all you could have done. If you lost, you lost. White people have a fine line, that line between sticking up for yourself and acting like a nigger."

Charlotte's mouth snapped open, and her face burned. Her mother never spoke such language.

"Unh-huh," her mother said slowly, deeply, like a low church hum. "That's right. I said it." She took Charlotte's face in her cool hands. "That's life. You have no choice, have to touch that hot iron. Got to feel the heat."

AT 106 DEGREES, CHARLOTTE and Heath can only brace themselves against the Nevada winds whipping across their faces. There's no relief from it, though Charlotte has decided that the misery of it is worth the panoramic canvas of red, brown, and purple mountains stacked up against each other, surrounding the casinos. After tipping the valet and backing out of the Monte Carlo parking lot, Heath has decided that Charlotte is hungry too. "I didn't see you eat anything," he says. "You *have* to be."

Charlotte shrugs. "Sure. That's fine. But you're just trying to put off the splendor and the glory that is Liberace."

"Something is wrong with you," Heath says, grinning. He stares straight ahead, keeps his eyes on the road, but works his free hand under Charlotte's black skirt. "You just aren't right." He pulls his hand out from under her skirt and smooths it back to its original placement. "Pretty," he says. "I look downright shaggy next to you."

"You're sweet, Shaggy," Charlotte says, placing her hand on top of his. She gives it a squeeze. "Let's eat."

There is debate, but finally Charlotte agrees to the restaurant Heath wants to go to. It's fancy—Vegas fancy, and a chain, but still. Heath isn't dressed right. He's wearing an old R.E.M. concert T-shirt frayed around the neckline from too many washings. And filthy flip-flops, with the dirt of all his travels covering what used to be the flip-flops' white soles. He didn't even shower. They are only having lunch, but still, Charlotte considers all of this. And the more she looks at Heath, she isn't even sure if she's appropriate, not sure she'd fit, either.

"I'll let you out," Heath says. "There's a line. You put our names in, and I'll be right there."

Charlotte hesitates but then unlocks the door. She hates being the one to put her name in at restaurants, hates being the one to ask when her name will be up, hates being the one to always be asking, *How much longer?* When the people running the place, pick a place, any place, will always say, just a few more moments, and leave you waiting—and waiting—it seems. Charlotte looks at Heath's torn shirt and then tugs at her tank top.

"Hey. There's people behind us. Hurry up," Heath says.

"Are we dressed okay?"

"You're kidding, right? Tacky is as tacky does. When in hell," Heath says, gesturing toward the array of flip-flopped, T-shirted tourists ambling along the sidewalks.

"I'll park with you. Then you can put our names in."

"Charlotte," Heath says. "Sweetheart. Now's not the time for that thing you do. I'm hungry. I'm hot. I'm in a hurry to get you to the goddamn Liberace Museum so we can get out of here. Just get out, go in, and place our names. Ask for a booth, too." He taps the steering wheel with his thumbs, tilts his head toward the door. "Chop, chop, Charlotte."

Chop, chop. He always ends a request with that phrase, turning it into a command, a verbal snap of the fingers, *now, not later*, with the authority of someone who has no doubt that B will follow A, ask and you shall receive.

Charlotte gets out of the car.

IN THE RESTAURANT, JUNGLE-THEMED, amid a concert of birds and insects provided in surround sound, Charlotte's name is taken by a young woman named Tiffany. It says so on her name tag. And then, after Charlotte's name is taken, she waits. Incredible, she thinks, spotting birds here and there, camouflaged in the vines. She'll make a joke about jungle fever when Heath returns, and even he will finally appreciate the irony of this place. The restaurant walls have a thin sheet of water spilling down them, pleasant trickles and gurgles everywhere she turns. The lighting is natural—man-made to look natural—as though she's standing in the middle of the Amazon, daylight shifting into twilight. She looks at her watch. Only two minutes have passed. She looks at the vines, lush and strangely lifelike, hanging from the ceiling. Five minutes. Where is

Heath? Four people in line behind her have been seated. *They need a bigger table, that's all. Not a table for two.* Ten minutes. Charlotte begins to feel invisible. Or does she make herself invisible? The thing she does, the thing that drives Heath crazy, is this: She dreads. The thing she dreads is the thing that happens, is the thing she shrinks from, is the thing she may make happen by shrinking from it. If it could happen once—and it has—it could happen again. People sued, they did, because it was still happening. The fear of it happening, that's what paralyzed Charlotte, made her stand still as a statue, something you only noticed if you were looking, truly looking; made her contain herself, compose herself because she might make a spectacle of herself, might ask Tiffany to her expertly tanned face, "What in the fuck is taking so goddamn long?" Does she ask what's taking so long? Or does she wait, politely, as taught to do? *Don't call attention to yourself.* As expected? Finger wagging and neck gyrating at every little thing? *Blend. Act your age, not your color. Don't say things like that, Mom.* Does she want to be seen? Or not? Which is it? She has felt fury when asked, pointedly, if she "can be helped." A woman and a man who have come after Charlotte have just been seated. *For any number of reasons.* Pushing their whiteness out of her head. *Any number of reasons. It's just food. In a tacky restaurant. Stupid, stupid girl. You're an idiot. Idiot. Tiffany's an idiot. These people who sit down without a thought about the fact that they are sitting down, how they are sitting down, why they are sitting down, when I am still standing, are idiots. And even if they weren't sitting down, even if they were standing, as I am now, at least they would not be doing this, this thing I do, this endless loop, on and on this loop, all merely because Tiffany is slow, is absentminded, is a bad hostess, not because of anything else, anything else at all. So wait. It's nothing. You're crazy, you're silly. Calm down. Wait and stand still. You are a rock, a smooth and solid rock, flawless as marble.*

The door opens, and a burst of hot air warms Charlotte's skin. The jungle is air-conditioned.

"Hey. What's the matter with you?" Heath asks. She rubs her arms as if she's been burned. He's dripping sweat, and his face is bright pink as if he's just been through something exhausting.

"Nothing." She smiles at him and points to the ceiling. "Look. There are vines hanging from the ceiling."

Charlotte wants Heath to grin, but his mouth goes slack. "Good gracious. I'm near defeated. I can't take it anymore. We have to get out of here."

"Where? Where else is there to go?"

"I meant out of here, out of Vegas, straight to L.A."

"Oh." Charlotte takes a deep breath and lets it out slowly, patiently, and her body seems to relax in one fluid motion. "I thought you meant something else. Another country."

"Ha. The both of us, we'd last a day. Hopeless. About as American as they come," Heath says, "the kind of folks who need distractions like fake vines in our restaurants." He pokes her in her side. Charlotte agrees, though Heath is the one who is distracted enough to miss the joke, the obvious irony of the two of them in a jungle-themed restaurant, Heath burning up, hot to the touch. She thinks the vines are funny, has to turn them funny. And Heath is right. This is America, this tacky restaurant. No need to deny it.

"Ma'am?" Tiffany appears with overlarge menus tucked under her arms. "We're ready to seat you now. Be right with you, sir."

"We're together," Heath says, taking Charlotte's elbow and guiding her to their table. "See?" he rubs the small of her back as she follows Tiffany.

"The way you carry on sometimes. You walk in, you sit down, honey. It's that easy."

ALL HER LIFE, CHARLOTTE has been drawn to museums, and all her life, they have disappointed her. If she is near one, she seeks it out, imagining an opportunity to touch history, be touched by history. She wants to be transported, to feel the mark of history, the stain of history, so she can always carry this history with her and never forget. It is effortless, this forgetting, and Charlotte is always disappointed in herself. But somehow, this forgetting isn't all her fault—it is facilitated by the very presentation of history: nicely lit and neatly packaged. Once, at the Holocaust Memorial Museum in Washington, D.C., she stood in an actual train car that transported Jews to their death, well aware that she was not grasping the weight of the train, the horror of the train. Instead, she was preoccupied with the logistics of the train. Where did it come from? How was it transported to Washington, D.C.? At the Museum of Tolerance in L.A., she received a card with the statistics of a little French boy, which she carried with her until the end of the exhibit, at which time she'd find out if he was a survivor of the Holocaust. He wasn't. He stayed with her for a while, this boy, until she was out of the museum and realized that she'd dropped her card somewhere between finding out his fate and leaving the museum. Then she became preoccupied with wondering how she lost her card, her souvenir. At the Louvre, Mona Lisa barely gave up her smile behind the thick protective plexiglass, and Charlotte wondered then: Why plexiglass just for Mona Lisa, and not for all the other valuable art? Who decided that Mona Lisa was *the* most important part of art history? It was always the same, except once, at the Vatican Museum. After pulling down her skirt just far enough below the knee to gain entrance, she came the closest to history. She wandered around, overwhelmed by the fact that everything in the museum was framed by, set in, or cast in gold. She became lost in the presentation, could not grasp that any of it was real. *This wealth, these things, are real*, she kept telling herself, and yet she wasn't moved, not in the way she wanted to be. But as she was leaving, she noticed a marble sculpture. Three figures that looked like warriors writhing in pain and ecstasy, their paroxysm of emotion somehow captured and rendered in stone as pythons entangled and constricted them. Every detail, down to the muscles and veins in the captives' thighs, mesmerized Charlotte. She stared and stared until she'd convinced herself that their bodies would be warm to the touch—not hard, cold marble, but soft as skin. She stared at them until the warriors began to move, the pythons slithering between their legs, grazing the tip of one captive's penis while another threw his head back, exposing the pulsing vein in his neck, eyes rolled back in his head as if surrendering himself. Charlotte couldn't breathe; she felt as though she were being constricted, too. Whoever had made this sculpture, sometime in 50 BCE, had made history a living thing, told Charlotte something about pain and release. She repressed a sudden outburst, the impulse to cry out, held the back of her hand against her mouth and clutched her stomach. Faint, she stumbled out of the Vatican, where a young woman with a maple-leaf patch on her backpack asked Charlotte if she was okay. But Charlotte couldn't answer. She did not know.

SHE NEVER FIGHTS WITH Heath, but they fought the day they visited the Civil Rights Institute. Heath was insulted that Charlotte rushed through the museum, but she was sorry: Sure she was occasionally moved, but nothing destroyed her. That's what history should do, but she should have known. The things she saw and heard—the WHITES ONLY sign, audio of Martin Luther King Jr.'s "I Have a Dream" speech piggybacked by marchers singing "We Shall Overcome," a section of a bus that was used by freedom riders—all these things struck her as knowledge she'd already been well taught, like spelling drills and flash cards. And how did they get the bus inside the museum? Was it taken apart and reassembled? Is that how they did the train at the Holocaust Museum? In bed later that night, in one of the spare rooms of the "big house," as Charlotte had started to call it, Heath tried to explain why his feelings were hurt. He said that, in their relationship, they've had to talk and talk, in circles, about race, and now that he'd taken the initiative, taken her somewhere he thought would please her, she didn't care, didn't appreciate it.

Charlotte lay beside him, still as a statue, listening to him trying to reach her, trying to get to her. She felt heavy and cold. "How many times have you been to that museum?" she asked finally.

"Just once, not that it matters. I'm proud of what the South is offering with that museum." Heath turned over, his back facing her. "It's important, what people have struggled for."

"What about Sixteenth Street Baptist across the street from the museum? Those little girls blown up in it? Have you ever been inside?"

"Jesus." Heath breathed slowly. "No."

"Why not? They still have sermons there, don't they?"

"Yes, but."

Charlotte waited.

"It's a horrible, horrible thing."

"Yes it is," Charlotte said, and the word *horrible* meant nothing to her, sounded like a made-up word, like *hubba, hubba*. She pulled his shoulder so he would turn to face her. She didn't want to fight, not if it didn't get them anywhere. She wanted to be close to him. Closer.

"I'm sorry, Mr. Bolinger," she said. She climbed on him, and he lay flat on his back to accommodate her. She kissed his face, ran her hands along his belly. "Mr. Bolinger, I *do* appreciate everything you provide for me, sir."

Heath sighed. He stroked her face. Then he snickered. "Sir? That's more like it."

"Let me make it up to you."

"Go right on ahead, darlin." Heath put his hands on Charlotte's waist and ran his delicate fingers along her spine. "We have to be quiet. So my parents don't hear." The parents were far away, down a long corridor, on the other end of the house.

"Tell me something."

"*Yes*," Heath whispered, and he moaned when Charlotte put his cock in her hand. "What do you want me to tell you, darlin?"

"Say . . ." Charlotte whispered. "Say, 'I'm going to fuck you hard, you black whore.'"

Heath stopped breathing. Charlotte couldn't feel his chest rising and falling underneath her.

"Say, 'You like this white cock, don't you, you black bitch.'"

Heath was still. Frozen in place. "I will not," he said. "I can't say that. I would never disrespect you like that. I love you."

She tried again. "I love you too. That's the point. You never even *thought* it? Tell the truth. You've thought it."

"What point?" Heath turned his head. "I can barely stand you sometimes," he said. "Barely tolerate you." He wouldn't look her in the eyes. He pushed Charlotte off of him, rolled over, and pulled the covers close around his neck as if he were cold on that suffocating, hot evening. "I *told* you. I *said*. I would never *say* those things to you."

LIBERACE'S MUSEUM IS DOWN the street from the strip, doesn't look so grand yet, not from the outside. "Oh, I see," Heath says, as they make their way in and pay for their tickets. They're at the end of a long line, he and Charlotte. He looks around the Liberace Museum, clearly not impressed. The entrance is small, though Charlotte can see that it appears to get bigger. Pictures of Liberace line the blue walls, and piano music tinkles in overhead speakers. "The Civil Rights Institute is a snore, but this is valuable to our cultural history?"

"I said I thought it'd be funny. I never said it was the Vatican Museum or anything."

"Please," Heath says. "Talk about something going unsaid."

"You mean something going without saying."

"What," Heath says, checking his watch, "is the difference?"

THE TOUR GUIDE IS a tiny woman named Joannie with baubly earrings and long hair dyed black. She puts Charlotte in the mind of someone's kindly grandmother, with a bit of a spark. She stops the large group in the narrow entrance, amid several black-and-white photos of a young Liberace, looking demure and immaculate in conservative tuxedos, not a candelabra in sight, not in his early years. Charlotte has to stand on her tiptoes to get a good look, to see above all the heads. Joannie tells the group why the museum is located so far away from the strip. "It all boils down to not having enough money to take his rightful place on the strip," she says sadly. She shakes her head, and her silver earrings catch a glint of light. "If we had the money, we'd be right there with everyone else, where we belong." She is plucky and feisty. Charlotte smiles at her.

Heath blows an exaggerated breath and checks his watch again.

"The Liberace would get his due. Liberace is Vegas," Joannie says.

"We get it," Heath mumbles in Charlotte's ear. "Life and death, this little woman acts like."

Charlotte levels her eyes at Heath. He holds his hands up in surrender and makes the gesture of zipping his lip and crossing his heart.

As they shuffle through the tiny museum, broken up into two buildings, it is no surprise to Charlotte that she is disappointed.

The space seems too small; all of Liberace's cars are crammed together in the first room, and, in an adjacent room, the pianos all look dusty and used up, and a red velvet rope keeps the tour group from getting too close.

The group stands in the cramped room and listens dutifully while Joannie continues: "This rhinestone Baldwin grand piano matched his suit and his car." She caresses the piano lovingly. "He was criticized for the runs and flourishes he put into his performances, but he didn't care. He was known as Mr. Showmanship, and he was the first on TV to look straight into the camera."

"Goody for him," Heath says. He scratches his elbow, and Charlotte nods at Joannie as if she is getting important instructions. It's only right, good manners, to respect Joannie by paying close attention to her.

"Follow me to the next building," Joannie says. "To the costume room. You're really in for something now."

But Charlotte's ears and eyes are tired. The museum is lit so that all the light bounces off everything glittery. She keeps trying to blink stars out of her eyes while she hears endless Liberace facts: He owned ten homes, made millions, had dozens of capes—some mink, others feathered. The red, white, and blue sequined hot pants matched one of his cars in the other showroom, were designed to commemorate the two-hundredth anniversary of the Statue of Liberty. Charlotte has to admit that the costumes *are* spectacular. The hot pants, especially. She should be more amused, though. Instead, she is overwhelmed by the presentation, which turns into numbness. Joannie, bless her heart, is droning. When Heath catches her yawning, he raises his eyebrows, then wags a finger at her. Charlotte's eyes are droopy, and she feels sleepy, as if she's oxygen-deprived. Maybe it's because she's sleepy, or maybe it's because she and Heath are in the back rows of the tour group, but she doesn't notice at first the young man sitting at the rhinestone piano at the center of the room. Then there's the candelabra, which partially obscures him. In fact, when he scratches the tip of his nose, he startles her because he looks like a mannequin in a sequined white tuxedo, he's so perfectly still, so perfectly made-up and coiffed. He waits patiently while Joannie talks, and when Charlotte catches his eye, he winks at her.

"This room is the last room of the tour," Joannie says. "Here, we have my dear sweet boy, Mark. The son I never had." She blows Mark a kiss.

He pauses, waits for her kiss to reach him, and then grabs his chest as though he's been hit with it. Even from a distance, Charlotte can see that he's wearing a soft pink lipstick, accented with a shimmery gloss. "He's the winner in this year's Liberace Keyboard Entertainer Search, and today, he is going to play something lovely for you."

"You owe me," Heath says. "A man can only take so much."

Mark lays his hands on the piano keys gently, as if calming the room for a sermon. Charlotte moves in closer, grabbing Heath's belt loop so he will follow. She can see Mark's pinky piano ring glinting, the black eyeliner, and the rouge accenting his chiseled cheeks.

"I just want to say it's an honor for me to be here," Mark says. His voice is high and theatrical. "When I was a young boy in Oklahoma, I used to watch my grandmama's videotapes of Liberace, and he used to stare back at me and wink at me, and I would feel like I wasn't so alone in the world. I would feel like he was telling me, 'Mark, don't you worry none. Whatever you are, whatever you want to be, you be it.' Well, the kids would laugh at me because I was different, wanted to be like Liberace and let it all hang out."

The tour group laughs at this, and Charlotte can't take her eyes off Mark.

"So," Mark licks a finger and smooths down a sandy curl at his temple. More laughter. He pinches his cuff links as if checking his pulse. "Even though I was never taught formally, I did it my way. I let it all hang out, and I won me a scholarship. Beat out all those fancy boys and girls with years and years of training."

Everyone in the room applauds.

"But enough about me. You all are here for the master. Mr. Showmanship. And I'm going to play Joannie's favorite song just like Liberace himself might have played it—with my own flair, of course." He splays his fingers across his collarbone for emphasis. "She doesn't like me to play it so much because it makes her cry in front of you all, but she says she always feels good after hearing me play it, and I always feel good, seeing Joannie cry. I know I'm not going through the motions then, playing notes without feeling them. And when has Mr. Showmanship ever gone through the motions?" He gestures to the costumes lining the walls of the room.

More laughs. Mark chuckles, and his eyes scan the room. "So ladies and gentlemen, allow me." He pauses dramatically. "Memory." Someone coughs, and someone clears a throat.

Mark starts slowly and gently, then gradually builds up to ripples and flourishes in between notes. His hands fly up and over and across the piano keys, and in the small room the notes bounce off the walls resonant and clear. He closes his eyes and seems to lose himself, throws his head back so that Charlotte can see the vein in his neck glistening under the thin sheen of sweat that begins to cover his face. At first, Charlotte is embarrassed for Mark; he's so serious about what he's playing, not ironic at all, playing "Memory" as if his life depended on it, as if it wasn't one of the most over-played and overused songs in the history of music. But this is what she wanted; she's come to the museum for excess, and now she's nervous about this excess, watching Mark watching Joannie while he plays, feeling on the verge of something, as if something is going to happen, as if she will burst out laughing in the middle of this reverential room with all these people who will look at her, and across the room she sees Joannie, looking at Mark with love in her eyes, wringing a tissue in her hands, wrapping it around one hand like a tourniquet, putting the hand against her lips as though kissing herself, and Charlotte cannot watch anything but Mark and Joannie, likes the feeling she gets watching them, doesn't want Mark to ever stop playing his notes, doesn't want to stop feeling as though she is on the verge of something, as if something is going to happen, but Mark is slowing down, and Charlotte knows the song is going to end as he reaches the last notes and lifts his head and stares only at Joannie, and when Charlotte sees Joannie return his gaze, she sees something else, something that Joannie and Mark will never have to say to each other because they've both thought it or it's already been said, and if it hasn't already been said, it can't be said, to Joannie, to this boy, the son Joannie never had. Mark finishes "Memory" with a thunderous commanding note that reverberates in Charlotte's chest and stays in her ears long after it is played.

Mark nods gracefully, magnanimous and humble until the applause subsides. When Joannie walks up to Mark and places her hand on his shoulder, he stands up and puts his arm around her. "This is the end of the tour," she says. She turns to embrace Mark, kisses him on the lips, holds and holds him and doesn't let go. Her shoulders shake as he rocks her and whispers in her ear.

The group looks down at their shoes, at Liberace's fabulous costumes, at the large candelabra on Mark's piano, anywhere but at Mark, comforting Joannie, and slowly they begin to file out of the tiny room.

"Good God," Heath says as they make their way out into the gift shop, placed so customers have no choice but to pass through it. "Did I mention that you owe me big time? I'm telling you *what*. Did you *see* that pinky ring? And what was going on between *Joannie* and Mark?"

Charlotte stops walking. She doesn't want to buy any of it. None of it—not the rhinestone dog collars, the magnets, the mugs, the plaques—is worth carrying with her. She turns to face Heath, grips both his hands, looks him in the eyes. *Tell me what I'm thinking.* But he is at a loss, doesn't understand what is happening, doesn't understand why she is holding his hands so tightly, her face between them. "Sweetheart. What are you crying for, baby? That," Heath says, wiping a tear away with his thumb, "was hilarious."

SHE DESERVES EVERYTHING SHE GETS

W e are all sitting around the fire pit, talking about how not to get raped. We have advice, opinions, instructions because we are the adults and Gertrude is the kid, and we've been to college, so we think we know what we are talking about. She lets us talk at her all night, ruining her graduation present because she's an exceptional kid, an obedient kid. She's not an eye roller. She doesn't text while people are trying to talk to her. She's not the kind of kid you'll overhear calling somebody a cunt or her mother a bitch. *Whatever* is not in her vocab. She's super adjusted and polite and so "she deserves everything she gets," her parents say *all* the damn time. And this kid gets a lot. Always has. Therefore, like an idiot, she believes that everything in her life, her brand-new Prius, her house that her parents bought for her so she could have a place to live when she gets to college, this vacation to San Diego, *because she saw a picture of the house and the beach in a fucking magazine*, and everything leading up to this moment, sitting in front of a fire pit with explicit instructions on how not to get raped, all of this, is what happens to people who are good. "Why does she get under your skin?" her uncle, my husband, is always asking me. "It's not normal," he says. He thinks it's because I'm middle-aged. That I'm jealous of her flat stomach and eyes with no bags underneath. Her ability to do the splits. "Jealous of a teenage girl," he says. "You really need to figure that out." And then I roll my eyes and say, "Whatever."

TALKING ABOUT RAPE IS something we can do because her little sister and brother are in bed now, upstairs, tucked away in their kids' room, the ceiling and walls blanketed with stars, the universe at their fingertips. Because it's Southern California, the day started out warm and the night is cold. The fire pit is nestled in the front yard, which jets out toward the San Diego ocean, which nobody can see because of the fog that's rolled in. We can hear it though, big waves coming in like big feelings, roaring and then breaking up, like talking big, big shit with nothing to back it up. Catastrophic crashes turn to hisses you can barely hear, but still. You hear.

Gertrude's dad is drunk, so he's starting to talk to his daughter like a bro, saying stuff like, "Some dude, some rando, is going to try to hook up with you, and you need to know what to do—"

"I know," Gertrude says. She nods, and her red ponytail sways all over the place. "You can trust me."

"He'll try to put something in your drink—"

"Give you a roofie," her mother says, tilting up a Corona and then putting it down with a loud clink.

My husband, her uncle, says, "Do not, under any circumstances, let some asshole buy you a drink. Get your own drinks. Tell him you've got your own money and that you could buy him drinks for a year, if you wanted to. You know why?"

"Because. I know. Mom already said."

"You have to be really, really careful," I say. Nobody's ever tried to give me a roofie, not that I know of. I'm talking out of my drunk ass. "Never trust somebody who says they're going to take care of you. Nine times out of ten, they're full of shit."

BECAUSE GERTRUDE IS GOING to college, everyone wants to reminisce. Her father is big on his frat days, nights of drunk driving and puking and hooking up that he now warns his girl not to do, ever. *Ever*. Her mother is all about her student activism, Students for Peace and Justice, Take Back the Night. To me, college is overrated. It's not what I thought it was going to be, not at all. Gertrude asks me, "What was your favorite part about college?" I say, "Let me think for a minute," and I stare at all the faces around the fire, underlit like something spooky. And the fog, so sneaky, looking thick out in the distance, as if it hasn't settled in all around us, invisible up close but there just the same.

"SHE LIKED THE MUSIC," my husband says after a while, even though he didn't know me then, but he's right. I did. I forgot about that.

"The '80s were the best," Gertrude says. She is, in fact, wearing the same enormous ugly tortoiseshell glasses that I wore in college, only because I had no choice. That's all we had to choose from, me and Josefa, my best friend. We couldn't afford lenses that didn't jut out inches from your face, like binoculars. They call girls like we used to be "outliers" now, and they mean that word as a compliment. Back then, it just sucked. We did not know who we were, me and Josefa. Josefa, who didn't want to go to college but who needed to go to college with me. I was a freshman. I had filled out all the forms to get in myself, not like now. The parents fill out everything. Josefa didn't want to bother. "I'm never going to get in," she said. So I was a freshman and she wasn't. "Just come for the weekend," I told her. "I can't," she said. "I have to work." "Bullshit. One night. I got your back." And so she came to college.

I WAS GOING TO show Josefa everything she was missing out on, and all the things I wanted for her were the things that she deserved. But for now, like me, that night she had nothing, coming off a bus and into the apartment with her clothes in a little plastic grocery bag, like a hobo out of a Steinbeck novel. All that was missing was the stick. She came from the San Gabriel Valley, from a job bagging groceries and pushing shopping carts at Stater Bros. The job I had was no better, asking people if they wanted fries with that. Still, I had more sense than Josefa. I understood, at least, that a job asking people questions about French fries was not the kind of job you were supposed to keep. By the time she rang the bell, everything had already started. People were roaming around the apartment I shared with my roommate, María Fernanda, sitting on her couch, playing their Rick James and R.E.M. on her tape deck. María Fernanda. I made the mistake of calling her just María at first. "It is both," she said. "Both names together."

I say *her* couch because it was her couch, truly. She hadn't liked the green plaid couch that came with the apartment, a couch that had accommodated the asses of college students for a decade. She had moved in days after I had, tall, all wild hair and gold bangles. She glanced at the couch and sucked her teeth. "This is very ugly," she had said, in perfect English she'd learned, she said, from watching episodes of *The Three Stooges* when she came to California from Bogotá. Two days later, the saggy plaid couch was gone and there was a new, streamlined couch in its place. White. I didn't sit in it. Her guests sat in it like they lived there. I was watching them from the kitchen, stuffing my face with Cheetos. There was a guy who looked like

Boy George, and that was novel back then, the guts to go around looking like that in real life, like a man and a woman with multicolored dreadlocks, the hair of a black person. I was so happy to see Josefa, peering in through the cracked door, not sure if she was in the right place. All the apartments looked the same: street level, a cluster of oatmeal-colored stucco, bleached by the sun. She stepped inside and stared. Her eyes landed on Boy George, like some country girl seeing city sights, and it's true, nobody in the valley—that we knew—would have dared. Our moms didn't work hard so we could go around looking like nobody had raised us.

Josefa weaved through the people, so short she came up to most of the guys' waists, and dropped her plastic bag on the kitchen floor. She had a big red bow in her hair that was partially lost in the big frizz of it. I hugged her, took her into my room—bare, except for a bunk bed, a squat brown desk with the wood laminate peeling away, and a poster of the Smiths standing in front of a brick arch somewhere in England. I put her plastic bag deep into my closet, in the corner behind my basket of dirty clothes, because we came from a place where people took things all the time if you didn't take precautions.

"So you're here," I said.

Josefa nodded. "That couch," she said. "How long is it supposed to stay white?"

I shrugged, rolled my eyes. "She'll just get another one if that one gets ruined," I said. I thought I was going to say it like my roommate was stupid for wasting her money like that. But I was bragging.

Josefa reached up and fluffed her bow. She straightened her back. "Let's go stare at Boy George."

•

"WE ARE ALL SO proud of you," Gertrude's father says. "You never gave us any trouble."

"You're the kind of kid who could go anywhere," his wife says. "Paris. Morocco."

She looks at me and my husband, full of wonder. "Gertrude was like, 'Mom, look at this house. Isn't it beautiful? It's a vacation home, it says. That's what I want. For graduation. That house. For two weeks.' I couldn't believe it. Any other kid would have asked for the moon. Instead, we get San Diego. A six-hour drive from home."

I glance at my husband, who seems to have been watching me very carefully during this speech. But my face? My eyes aren't telling him anything.

He asks, "You want some more champagne?"

THE COLOMBIANS WERE COMING, that's why Josefa had to come *that weekend, seriously.* Those were my words. They were María Fernanda's cousins, and she was something else that I never imagined about college, the kind of person you never know because she's never around, except when, suddenly, there are people in your apartment drinking, dancing, and talking loudly. Having, technically, a party. María Fernanda was bored by me, that I understood. I could not talk to her about the things she liked to talk about, the places she'd been, the ski trips or river rafting. Who *did* these kinds of things? Get in a tiny rubber boat and paddle against enormous waves? Banish offensive couches? Now she was having a party and had invited these cousins, who I had seen in pictures. In small frames, they looked handsome, the three brothers. In one silver frame, the brothers had made a pyramid out of themselves, but they were collapsing, the smallest brother caught falling from the top, all of their faces dimpled in laughter. Josefa had to be there. I was going to make her fall in love with college. We were not going to be like our mothers, holding down *jobs*, plural, something that always sounded to me like our mothers were wrestling with men out to get them.

THE FLAMES OF THE fire pit suddenly flare up, scare me, until I realize it's my husband behind me. He has stopped just outside the front door to turn up the fire.

"Getting aggressive there, bud," his brother says. "How much fire do we need?"

"Just enough," my husband says. He grins when his reading glasses fall from the top of his thinning red hair and onto his nose.

I watch the flames grow taller and dance like crazy demons.

"Madame," my husband says, handing me a clean glass of champagne. The first one, he'd taken away because it had collected my fingerprints. It's a habit I have. I want a clean glass after a while. I don't like to see my smudges and lipstick on glass, looking dirty, so anyone can see.

Gertrude is bundled up in a blanket, looking freshly scrubbed. Her mother is staring glassy-eyed into the fire. We all are. What is it about fires and the need to look directly into them? We're all getting quiet. Maybe it's the beer and wine and bourbon. Maybe it's the fog. Gertrude yawns. "Somebody should tell a ghost story," she says. Her father starts to tell the one about the hitchhiker, which everyone has heard, which no one can remember not having heard, the one where you think you're picking up a person, but you're picking up a ghost, and the ghost gets picked up over and over again. Who picks up strangers anymore?

•

THEY WERE THREE BROTHERS, in sequence according to height, and they always stood like that, at the party, slanting from tallest to smallest. The tallest one was balding, with a big smooshy nose. The middle one had hands that were way too small and soft and moist when he shook my hand. The last one, the youngest, had green eyes and hands that were just right, of tolerable size and toughness. He liked Josefa, I could tell from my spot in the kitchen, the way he followed her around, delivering Jell-O shots on command. She kept swallowing the shots like they were food, and even though I didn't know it then, now I know: That is *not* the thing to do.

When she came into the kitchen for water, I grabbed her hand. "Do you like him?" I wanted her to like him. I smiled at her with raised eyebrows, willing her to love him for her own good. Josefa looked at me through eyes that were just slits. "He's cute," Josefa said. "I like him all right, I guess. He wants to be a doctor. He told me he gave CPR to his maid once."

"It's good!" I said. "You're Mexican. He's Colombian. It's perfect." Josefa laughed at me. "You think they're the *same?*" When she walked away, she looked back at me and laughed again. As she walked away from me, down the hallway, her fingertips carefully stroked one of the white walls. This is what I saw: ski trips and river rafting, elegant dinners on long wooden tables in the countryside, tablecloth billowing in the wind. I saw so many things, but whatever I saw did not exist.

After a while the night got weirder. Someone turned down the lights. The music was louder, but somehow the room was quieter. I saw mostly pairs of people, and I saw María Fernanda on the floor between two guys. I saw a guy with long blond hair sitting, just sitting very quietly on a chair, and then slowly, very slowly, vomit started to trickle from his mouth. "Hey, man," someone said. He patted him on the back. "Gross, dude. You okay?" But I left them after a long time of waiting in vain for someone to put his sloppy drunk hands on me. It had been forever, it seemed, and so I went looking for Josefa. There were only three rooms for her to be in. I checked the bathroom first. I knocked on the door. Someone pulled me in. It was Boy George and another guy. "Watch us kiss," he said, and so I did. And then, Boy George kissed me. He licked my face, and his tongue felt like a cat's. "I thought you were gay," I said, and he laughed. His red lipstick was smeared all over my mouth, my chin, my cheeks. I wiped and wiped, but when I checked my hands, all of the red was still there. I went into the next room. One of the brothers was there, sitting alone. The balding one. He held something out to me, a silver flask. "Drink this," he said, and so I did. He held the flask up to my mouth, and I drank. "Ewww." I remember that's what I said. And he said, "This is the best Scotch money can buy. You don't know anything." But I knew. I knew it was disgusting. I left him sitting there, and then I went to the last room. I opened the door. Slowly, slowly. Josefa was on the bottom bunk, and the youngest brother was bending over her. I heard her moan. "Is she okay?" I stepped into the room, but he held his hand up like a policeman. "She's fine," he said. "Close the door." "Ungh," Josefa said. But I wasn't sure what to do, wasn't sure what was happening. He seemed to be taking care of her, watching over her. But it was very dark with just a little light coming in from the hallway. I listened. She wasn't crying. She didn't call out my name. "She's fine," the youngest brother said.

THE MAN SITTING NEXT to me, my husband who brings me clean glasses, I sold him a house. That's how we met. I was all hair-bun and business, wearing high heels that punished the hardwood floors. Stomping around like a constant exclamation point. I sold him a huge castle of a house in West L.A., where I had gone to school, an outlier who rose up to sell people houses with more room than they need. I sold his best friend a loft Downtown, in a building that was abandoned just ten years ago, where people squatted, no lights, no running water. "My wife the real-estate mogul," my husband likes to brag.

"I'M READY FOR BED," Gertrude says, shivering. She has to get up early for surfing. She pushes her ugly glasses up the bridge of her nose and stands.

"We've bored her," her mother says. "But she needs to know—"

"I know, I know, I know. Don't get raped," and then she hugs each of us, me last. I grab her by the wrist as she turns to go, and she looks down at my brown hand. I say, "I hope you were listening to your parents. I mean, *really* listening."

"I was," Gertrude says. "Don't I always?" Her lip curls up in one corner. Smiling back at her, I think, *You little bitch. You're not as simple as we think you are. Good for you.* Then her face goes solemn again, wide-eyed and innocent. She walks into the house and up the stairs, into a room that is all white, with billowy curtains.

TWO CRAZY WHORES

After a sixty-dollar taxi ride from Downtown to LAX, a taxi that lurched because the driver, a burly, chatty man, couldn't seem to keep even pressure on the gas—accelerating, and then releasing, accelerating, releasing, until Valarie had to take deep breaths to fight off car sickness—after the smell of cigarette smoke combined with tangy body order and pine-ish smelling air freshener, the too-loud radio station that played offensively bland jazz-ish music, after all that and suffering the tedium of being a part of the barefoot throngs re-buckling belts, reinserting laptops, and slipping back into shoes, here she was, finally, fidgeting on a plane, first class, bound for Paris, trying to shake off a bad attitude. *This is a luxury*, she reminded herself. This was not ordinary, this gift. Not Paris. Paris was ordinary; she had been many times, coming in late August and September, to avoid the crowds. Not first class. That, too, had become ordinary. But to be alone. To be one's self, not having to answer to anyone or be in charge of anyone. Alone, soon to be shooting through the sky like a glinty star. That was the gift.

She sat at the window seat, looking down at luggage being taken from silver carts and put somewhere in the belly of the plane. She had all of her distractions out for the long trip, a book—a mystery about yet another disappeared girl—her phone, in case she wanted to listen to music, and her iPad, for everything else. She checked her phone once more, to see if there was a text or voicemail from her daughter. There was not. There was not. There was not, Valarie accepted, after checking again. That little bitch. Let her know everything. Let her know everything and then suddenly not know a damn thing about the world. That will teach her.

She heard giggling. Three generations of women paused in front of her. They were related—same eyebrows, same noses, though their coloring differed. The mother of the teenager, Valarie guessed, was the lightest of the three, nearly white. Her mother was the darkest, and the daughter was somewhere in between, with a creamy butterscotch complexion. The mother and grandmother were impeccably put together, silver jewelry on the wrists, blazers, sleek hair and classic red lipstick. But the girl. The girl's hair was wild. And she was wearing pajama bottoms. Why had they let this child leave the house with uncombed hair, in pajamas?

"Mama, where you want to sit?" the mother of the teenager asked. "With me or over there?" She pointed her chin toward Valarie. Her mother chose quickly. "I'll sit with you." Valarie felt a flash of Wasn't-She-Good-Enough-to-Sit-Next-To? Like someone had glanced her way at the lunch table and kept walking. These people didn't even know her, so she told herself to knock it off— her daughter would accuse her of making where total strangers sat all about her and not *their* choices—but then, when the teenager sat down next to her, she felt a little like family. Four black women in a row, on their way to Paris. Still she was stuck, as she so often felt, with a teenager. The girl did not look at her. She put in her earbuds and hugged the large bear that doubled as a pillow. It was threadbare, the teddy bear, and the color had faded. The brown eyes had a dull, cloudy veneer that didn't match the exaggerated, empty grin or the nose in the shape of a heart. Why was a girl so old making a teddy bear pillow her travel companion? Valerie turned her head to look at the girl, waiting for the opportunity to say hello and make small talk. *You going to Paris, huh? Vacation?* But the girl never looked her way. So Valarie settled in her seat, drank the champagne that had been given to her by a charming flight attendant who seemed to float by, her hair in a perfect bun, lipstick on point, though a little smudged in the corners of her mouth, calling forth from Valarie two pleases and three thank-yous, she was so taken with the niceties. She ignored all the stuff about oxygen masks and emergency exits and following the lighted way should the plane lose power, so happy to put her life in some-body else's hands. Next to her, the girl had settled in with a game on her phone. In side-glances, Valarie saw shifting shiny pieces of candy that throbbed and shimmered until they were crushed into gray poofs of smoke. And sometimes, the shifting candy conjured up lightning.

The flight attendants walked by and closed overhead compart-ments with satisfying, hearty clicks. At last, they were on their way to Paris. Company work, sure. She would have to wear her fashion-buyer hat most of the time. She would have to think about lingerie and shoes and belts and jewelry. Talk to consultants and attend fashion shows, trade shows, and meet sales representatives. Look at all the lines. So much of her life is, will be, clothes—who's going to buy them, who will look good in them. But for now, she thought of sidewalk cafés and omelets cooked just so, of wine glasses filled with rosé or champagne. The plane rolled down the runway, would soon be leaving behind a streak of fumes. And then, it was the moment she could never guess, the only moment she truly dreaded on flights, when, if she did not focus on something right in front of her, Valarie would feel all over her body a crawling sensation that scrambled the insides of her stomach and made her want to laugh or cry, the moment she was no longer on the ground. The moment of liftoff.

Out of habit, Valarie checked her phone again, not really expecting a text from her daughter, who said she couldn't stand her, said Valarie was always in her face, said Valarie was such a fucking bitch. And ooh, how good a slap across her daughter's face would have felt. She wanted to slap her again and again. But she would never. Instead, she had said, "Who do you think you're talking to? This is *not* some TV show where the kids talk to their parents all crazy and out of their minds. My eyes are on you. My eyes are always going to be on you. You better straighten up." And her daughter had stomped out of their house, heavy with mystery and secrets, with the timeless threat of going to live with her father, the scent of weed and sex and the cloyingly sweet French perfume that Valarie had brought back as a gift from her last trip to Paris trailing behind her, a flash of a red mini-kilt and Doc Martins before the door slammed shut.

Valarie put in her earbuds, sipped her second glass of champagne, and listened to songs from an album she had downloaded: *Mullets Rock!* All the music she loved and grew up on. Jess had made fun of her, Loverboy taunting them on the ride home from school, the lead singer jeering, *You want a piece of my heart? You better start from the start.* Jess hadn't been able to take it. "Mom. Seriously?"

"You want to be in the show?" Valarie had sung at her daughter. "Come on, baby, let's go!"

"You would think," Jess had said, pulling her hands through her natural hair, which was parted on the side and textured with the perfect waves Valerie had taught her to do, "that you would have grown out of that phase by now."

"But when you're a mother, you can never be immune to nostalgia," Valarie had said, and Jess had said, "This was before you were a mother. What does old-people's rock have to do with me?"

Settled in her chair with her eyes closed, lyrics wormed themselves into Valarie's ear. *Mississippi queen, if you know what I mean . . . stroke me, stroke me . . . hot blooded, check it and see . . .* until Valarie was seduced into sleep.

AT FIRST, VALARIE THOUGHT she was in a dream. But it was just a fog. She had dozed. She'd fallen asleep, and now Cheap Trick was warning her. *Surrender, surrender, but don't give yourself away.* And there was something else sounding angry and muffled. She paused the song, took out her earbuds, and took in the white noise of the plane and the glow of the screen in front of her face, a little airplane attached to a line as it made its mechanical way overseas. The girl next to her was not asleep, and her earbuds were not stuck in her ears. But she was still on her phone, tapping it, stretching open images with her thumb and forefinger, swiping her fingers over it and looking intently into the screen as though she wanted to jump into it.

"I'm done." There was a voice, but Valarie didn't know where it was coming from.

"Thirty-five thousand dollars down the drain. You think you're grown, but you're not."

And then the girl mumbled something that Valarie could not understand. Her mother. It was the girl's mother who was talking.

"You waited until now to tell me this shit? What the fuck is wrong with you? Two times you flunk out?"

The girl mumbled again, but Valarie was still trying to understand what was going on.

"Your friends don't give a fuck about you. Texting those nasty boys at two in the morning. If you were grown, you'd handle your business. Wouldn't be flunking out of school again and again."

There was silence and no stirrings or acknowledgement from anyone else on the plane, making Valarie think everything she was hearing was not what she was hearing. For a long time, nothing was said. The girl stopped playing on her phone, sipped her orange juice, and stared at the movie playing on the screen before her, a cop show with people jumping out of windows and over roofs. Valarie looked at the little cup with foil peeled back, the kind she used to give Jess when she was little, and regretted that she had missed service. She sat up straight and stretched her neck, looking for a flight attendant, but she didn't she anyone. She would put the words away then, think about it as a strange thing that had happened, within a context that had nothing to do with her.

"You're just nasty. A straight-up whore. You're not Howard material, I know that much. Ruining my goddamn vacation with this shit. I think you may be crazy."

Valarie placed a hand over her stomach, to calm it. A warmth traveled from her stomach to her lower belly, and she thought she may have to get to the bathroom in a hurry. But she sat still. It was best to let what was happening blow over. If she stood now, she would embarrass the girl and her mother. Instead, she would hide in plain sight. Be quiet, until it all went away. Valarie leaned over, just a bit, just to get a look at the woman who would talk to her daughter this way. The grandmother was sitting back in her chair, eyes closed and unmoving, as if she wasn't hearing a thing. And the mother. The mother was not looking at her daughter at all, but looking forward, as if she were talking to the screen in front of her. Valarie finally turned, full body, to look at the girl, but the girl was still staring ahead too, watching cops without sound, as if this was the most normal conversation in the world, up in the air, amid strangers, in the glowing womb of the cabin. No one else stirred. Valarie sat back, fighting off the impulse to grab this girl's hand, fighting off a helpless feeling. She could say something. She could say, "Don't talk to your kid that way." She could say, "What are you teaching her?" She could say, "You're ruining her." She could say, "Are you all right, honey?" But the girl would get off the plane and move out into the world with her life already behind her and ahead of her, with her mother forever in her skin and cells and blood. Valarie felt something big, a memory. There was nowhere to go, nothing to do, but to sit there and take it, take in the memory. Nobody was going to help them, sitting there together, and how long would this last? The two of them in the dark, two whores. Two crazy whores. Forever. That's how long it would last. Valarie was still in a fog. She knew she was awake. She knew where she was. But she was also somewhere else.

SHE HELD HER FINGER up to her lips, saying, without saying, *Shhh. Dude. If you move, we're fucked.* And Gabs had moved anyway, pulling a shoe out from under her, quiet, calm and slow, like removing a card from a card house. She adjusted her coke-bottle glasses, framed in heavy tortoise shell. One eye looked tiny and one normal-sized because the tiny eye had the thicker lens. She looked at Val for clues on what to do because they were sitting in the closet, in Crazy Kate's room, hiding out, because Crazy Kate's dad was home. It was Crazy Kate's idea, to come over after school and play records and raid the fridge. It seemed like a good idea in the moment, and they had walked to Crazy Kate's house, blowing big Bubble Yum bubbles and being as loud as they could in their quiet neighborhood. All the houses looked dark inside, their windows a collective of closed eyes, which gave the girls permission. But now they were stuck. Val and Gabs were not allowed to hang out because they were a bad influence, Crazy Kate's dad said. But *their* parents said that they were not to hang out at Crazy Kate's house because *she* was the bad influence, with her jeans so tight you could see her you-know-what, and her makeup just cakes of blue and green and purple, making her blue eyes so big they took up her whole face. She drank too. And smoked pot. And climbed out her window at night. And fucked guys. Their parents didn't even know the half but still called her a crazy white girl. Valarie and Gabby loved her though, because she was a bad ass, and they weren't. Their leashes were short. "You guys need a trip slip just to take a dump," Crazy Kate always said, pointing and laughing at them. "Your mamas walk you to school every morning," she always said. "No they don't," Gabby would say. "They drive us." But Crazy Kate's parents kept her on a short leash too, especially her dad. Crazy Kate just chewed that leash up and shit on the carpet every time, she said. "My mom's an idiot," she would say. "She's so fucking blind, man. And don't even get me started on my dad. Don't talk to me about him." Her dad was the one that thought Gabby and Val were bad for Crazy Kate. In 1981, they were ruining the neighborhood just by being there. Their houses, side-by-side, too much black in one place.

They were scared, though. They weren't supposed to be there. One minute in the closet, and Val had already resolved to listen to her parents forever if she got out of this. If she had listened to them, she wouldn't be sitting in the dark, smelling sour dirty shoes and clothes. Through a crack in the sliding door of the closet, Val could see amber sun streaming through the shutters of Crazy Kate's window, and dust swirled around in the light like in a fairy-tale. They had been hanging out. Listening to music, laughing at Billy Squier singing "stroke me, stroke me," when Crazy Kate heard someone coming through the front door. "Get in the closet," she said, not even in a panic. She just said it like it was the right thing to do for the moment. And they would be all right, as long as Crazy Kate's dad didn't know they were there. "Don't say shit or come out until I tell you to," Crazy Kate said. She took the comb out of her back pocket and ran it through her gray-looking feathered hair, and then pushed them in and slid the door closed.

She left the room, and they heard muffled talk and then raised voices coming from down the hall. "No I'm not!" "I won't!" "I'm not going to!" And then they heard, "Go to your room," and footsteps, but they could tell that it wasn't just Crazy Kate that was coming.

Now, Val and Gabs huddled together the closer the steps got. They even held each other's hands, and Gabs squeezed her eyes shut, willing herself invisible. Crazy Kate and her dad were in the room now, not saying anything. Valarie heard the creak of the bed being sat on once. And then again. She and Gabs were still, trying not to breathe. Outside of the closet, no one said anything. Val wanted to look. It was too quiet. What was going on? She almost put her eye up to the small crack between the closet door and the wall, but she didn't. Crazy Kate's dad might see her, and then what?

Crazy Kate said, "Leave me alone! God!" and then her dad said, "I am tired of telling you the same things over and over again, Katherine."

Val looked at Gabs and mouthed, *Katherine*? Crazy Kate called Gabriella *Gabs*, and Val *Valley Girl*, but this *Katherine*, they had never heard of her. *Katherine* sounded old, like somebody's mother. She raised her eyebrows to make it into a question, and Gabs shrugged. She could picture Crazy Kate's dad. He wore a suit and tie to work. He was an accountant, and he always wore a shining silver watch. His suits were real suits, the kind made by tailors, from scratch, handmade with rich material. Not JCPenny. Not Sears, where her parents bought everything. She thought he was handsome, like a father on TV, with a deep voice and angry green eyes. His hair was a gray crew cut. "Your dad's kind of hot," Val had said to Crazy Kate once at lunch. "Gross," Gabs had said, splitting a Twinkie into three parts and giving the other pieces to Val and Crazy Kate. Crazy Kate had thrown Gabs a fierce look. "Fuck you, Gabs," she said. "That's my dad," and then she screwed up her nose and turned her lips into an ugly frown. She threw her head back, laughing a crazy laugh. "You want him? Valley Girl?" she had said. "You can have him." And then she threw her Twinkie on the ground. "I can't eat that shit. I'm trying not to be a cow."

In the closet, though, Val was listening very hard. They could only hear the bed making pinging noises every now and then, like somebody just moving a leg or maybe leaning back.

And then: "Your mother and I, we know what's best for you. Don't you understand that? All this running around. You're not a whore. So stop acting like one." Gabs looked at Val and frowned. The downturned corners looked exaggerated on her round, other-wise-cheerful face. "All your little whore friends. Is this what those black girls teach you? Climb out of your window in the middle of the night?" Val looked at Gabs's angry face, but Val, she had to put her hand over her mouth so she wouldn't make noise when she laughed. Her body spasmed as she sat there, a tight, clenched ball. He was stupid, Crazy Kate's dad! It was an epiphany. Some parents knew stuff because they were older and wiser, like hers—who she would listen to forever and forever if she ever got out of this—but some parents did not. Crazy Kate's dad was a dummy. He didn't even know that two black girls who had never been touched were hiding in his closet and that his daughter didn't care at all about whether she was a slut or not. She was the only girl in school who didn't care, and she was the only girl in school who the girls—and the boys—were afraid of. She laughed at their little dicks and told everybody she *knew* they were little because she'd seen a lot in her thirteen years. Val understood, all of sudden, sitting in a closet, that

Crazy Kate's father didn't even know that she had fucked Jaime and Russell and Javier and Brody and Kurt and Stanley and Harry and Ronnie. That's not why she was a slut. She was a whore because she didn't want to do what her dad wanted her to do when he wanted her to do it.

The bed creaked again. "Come here," Crazy Kate's father said.

"I'm here! God."

There was a soft patting sound. "Here," Crazy Kate's dad said.

Val and Gabs looked at each other frowning. Gabs shrugged. She pushed Val on the shoulder gently. *Look*, she said with her push. Val shook her head. Gabs pushed her again. They were both able to move and be so still at the same time. It's what they'd learned.

Val moved her head, slowly, slowly, like someone out of a movie, peering out from around a corner. She moved until her left eye could see through the crack in the closet door. Crazy Kate was sitting on her father's lap. She was sitting on his lap with her arms crossed and lip stuck out, like she was five and not thirteen. Her father's arms were on her shoulders, moving up and down, and then Crazy Kate started to cry. Val remembered something. She remembered four years ago, when she went to sit on her father's lap, like always, like she was always able to do, since she had memories, and her father had pushed her off his lap, so hard, and so rough, like she had done something awful to him. "You're too old for that now," he had said, and she had stood in front of him, not knowing where to go and what to do. He kept his face on the television, watching a football game. And Val had stared at his face, wondering if he was playing a joke on her. Teasing. "Go on, now," he'd said, and he put a smile on his face. "Go on. Go play or something." But Val had gone to her room feeling like all she wanted to do was to fit on her father's lap, that yesterday she could, and the next day she couldn't, and the reason she couldn't was because she had done something wrong. She had stayed in her room, the curtains closed and the lights turned off for hours, feeling sick and waiting to feel better about herself. That was four years ago, and now her one eye was telling her that today, it was worse that Crazy Kate's father wasn't pushing her off his lap.

Gabs poked Val in the thigh. Her eyes said, *Well?* Val moved from the crack in the door and put a finger up to her mouth.

After a minute, there was the creak and sudden quiet, and Val guessed they were standing up. "If you're going to cry," he said. There were footsteps, and then they heard the hinges on the door squealing. "No," Crazy Kate's dad said. "Keep it open. I need to keep my eye on you."

Val and Gabs waited and waited for Crazy Kate. Val slid open the door until Gabs could see out from beyond the door, herself. Crazy Kate was wiping her eyes. She got down on her knees and put her face as close to Val as possible. They were almost kissing, and Crazy Kate's breath smelled like Strawberry Quik. She whispered, "You guys will have to stay in here for a while."

"All *day*?" Gabs said, pushing her glasses up. "My mom's going to kill me."

"Mine, too," Val said. "I can't stay in here. Are you crazy?" That was her thing to say. *Are you crazy?*

"Unless you want my dad to know you're in here," Crazy Kate said.

"The window?" Gabs said.

Crazy Kate shook her head. "He's right *there*. He'll *hear*." She put her palm on Val's high forehead and pushed her back into the closet. She slid the door closed with a bigger crack than the last time and slid Gabs's side open a crack so that Gabs would get some light, too, and then Val and Gabs sat in the closet for two hours, until Crazy Kate's mom got home from work. She had walked into the room, her curly perm too tight, and asked her daughter how she was. Then they heard the short clicking sound of Crazy

Kate's mother blowing her a kiss. "Oh, God, stop," Crazy Kate said. "What?" her mother said. "I just got here and you already hate me." "No," Crazy Kate said, "I hated you before," and she slammed the door behind her mother.

When the door was finally closed, Val and Gabs climbed out of the closet like old arthritic women, unbending their limbs in slow motion. Gabs stretched and yawned. She looked at her Mickey Mouse watch. "It's six," she said. "Holy cow am I in a mess. Let's go," she said, pulling on Val's lime green T-shirt.

Crazy Kate opened the window, sliding it too loudly so that it banged. They all froze. Listening. Then Crazy Kate nodded. "Go. Get out." She took off the screen and let it fall outside on the grass. Gabs climbed out first. It was hard because the window was high. She got stuck, not knowing whether to fall out headfirst or perch on the windowsill. When Crazy Kate tried to push her, Gabs hissed, "Wait. There's a cactus right *here*." She wasn't used to climbing out of windows. Val watched because she wasn't either. She decided to perch, because when Gabs fell out of the window headfirst, it sounded like it hurt. She was about to hoist herself up when Crazy Kate grabbed her arm. She pulled Val close again, breathing her strawberry breath on her. The glitter on her purple eye shadow sparkled and made her eyes look huge. Pretty. Crazy Kate was one of those pretty girls, Val thought, not for the first time. "Don't tell," she said, and Val didn't have to say anything. She only had to nod. *Don't tell* meant many things. It meant don't tell your mom and dad, don't tell the kids at school, and don't tell Gabs, who was the goodest girl of the three. Not even a hand job. Don't tell Gabs most of all, because she could go either way, say Crazy Kate had a thing for sitting on her father's lap or tell the kids at school that sometimes Crazy Kate's leash was super tight and not chewed up at all, or worse, she could feel sorry for Crazy Kate, who always said, "Sorry ain't worth shit."

•

THE FLIGHT ATTENDANT WAS asking the girl and Valarie if they wanted anything to drink. She asked them twice, Valarie had just realized, because neither one was paying attention. The girl asked for a Diet Coke in a soft voice Valarie could hardly hear, and then Valarie asked for an orange juice, just because seeing the girl's orange juice earlier had made her want one. The stewardess poured the juice in a glass, and Valarie said she wanted one like the girl's, in plastic. The flight attendant shook her head and smiled. "She must have brought that herself. Did you bring that yourself?" She looked at the girl, and the girl nodded, not addressing Valarie at all. And Valarie didn't know what she had been thinking. No plastic. This was First Class to Paris.

She leaned forward to look at the mother and grandmother across the aisle. They were looking over a magazine together, pointing at the pages and nodding in agreement. The mother leaned over the aisle, extended the magazine. "Look, Tasha," she said. "Isn't this cute? You might be able to find something like this in Paris." Valarie looked across the aisle at the picture. A model was hunched over, her hands on her hips, neck extended and head at an odd angle, like a periscope. She was wearing an unremark-able outfit, something that looked like a skirt and jacket in beige wool, a woman's CEO outfit, and Valarie couldn't imagine this pajama-wearing, wild-haired girl in anything like that at all. The girl giggled. It was a strange, high-pitched giggle that reminded Valarie of one of the cartoons Jess had watched growing up, a giggle that sounded automatic and obligatory, and Valarie won-dered where the mother's anger had gone. How could she be calling her daughter nasty one minute and pointing at a fashion spread the next? As if all that had happened in the dark had been erased? *Maybe*, Valarie thought, *I misunderstood.* "Projected or whatever," her Jess would say. But Valarie would never talk to her daughter that way.

Valarie pulled her own magazine from the seat pocket in front of her: the September issue of *Vogue*, her favorite issue of the year, the heaviest. It was four and a half pounds and 658 pages long. She read that somewhere. This time of year was her favorite time to get lost in those pages. Sometimes, but not often, she liked to remember when she was young and flipping through magazines like *Seventeen* and *Sassy*. What they meant to her. They took her any place she wanted to go. That day after being at Crazy Kate's, her mother was, of course, furious that she had not been home after school. She had not called from Crazy Kate's because she hadn't had the chance. All she did was what she could do, which was hurry home. Her mother had slapped her face and asked her where she had been. "You better had not been running around, trying to be fast," she had said, and Val couldn't tell her about being stuck in the closet for hours and about Crazy Kate sitting on her father's lap. What was that, even? Would she even believe her? Would she call her nasty for thinking that it was *something*? Would she call Crazy Kate's mother and explode everything? Would Crazy Kate's mom think they were all lying? Would Crazy Kate end up hating Val? There was too much to think about. So she lied. She said that, yes, she had stopped at the donut shop with a boy named Ricky, who wouldn't be caught dead with her because she wasn't hot enough and she wouldn't fuck him. "We just split a donut," Val said, and her mother told her to get out of her sight. Val had stomped to her room and closed the door, too hard. Her mother flung it open. "This is my house. My door. You don't slam my door." And then she walked away, leaving it open. But then, she came back. Her mother stood in the doorway and hugged herself. She said to Valarie, "I made macaroni and cheese, from scratch." It was Valarie's favorite.

All night, Val sat in bed, flipping through magazines, thinking, *One day, I will be gone a long way from here. I will be an elegant, sophisticated woman, a closet full of clothes. One day I won't live in Diamond Bar, California. I'll live in a neighborhood that's mine. One day, I'll live on a street that has sidewalks, streets that aren't empty all the time. One day I'll walk out of the house and I won't have to get a ride anywhere, because I will already be in the middle of everywhere, people all around me. I'll live in a cool apartment in L.A. or maybe even Europe, wearing beautiful clothes like these girls.*

THE GIRL NEXT TO her was done with her movie. She went back to being distracted by her phone. Valarie imagined what she could look like, put together. Her hair sleek, her young, taut body encased in a stretchy-but-tight pencil skirt. Just the right accessories, maybe a gold chunky chain, or no, one of the thin ones that were in fashion now, with the girls' first initial resting mid-chest. This was what Valarie was always trying tell her daughter. "If I had your body," she was always saying. "Your thighs." But her daughter hated everything that Valarie ever brought home for her to wear. She'd always alter it somehow, so that a perfectly nice and lovely plaid kilt would be cut so short that it skimmed her ass. And she'd pair it with torn-up Converse when a heel would have been gorgeous. Worse, lately she had shaved one side of her head and let the rest flop off to the side, a tacky magenta flame covering up one eye. She was such a beautiful girl, but she did everything she could to make herself the opposite of beautiful. It didn't have to be that way. They had the money. Valarie knew how to dress her, but she threw all of that away for a pierced tongue and a tattoo of a pinup girl on her thigh. "It's my body!" her daughter had screeched this last time. "Why are you always on my ass!" But Valarie had only tried to show her how stunning she was, her baby girl, her love, the love of her life. "I'm going to give you the world, my love," she had said, rubbing her nose against Jess's tiny little one, fifteen years ago, smoothing down the dark wispy curls on her little head in the bed they shared together in the hospital. Jess's dad, he was there, at the beginning, but he was different. He was already in love with his daughter, but his love was different from Valarie's, which came out with her daughter, swallowed the two of them up, and wrapped itself around and around them, until they were bound together in an invisible veil. This love was terrorizing. This love told her that she could try and try but she could never protect her daughter from life. The love, it filled her with a ferocity that she sometimes aimed at other people who didn't value her daughter and that she sometimes aimed at her daughter, who didn't, it seemed to Valarie, value herself. This last fight, Valarie had pulled her daughter's skirt down, and it ripped. "Everybody knows you have an ass," Valarie had said. "Why do you feel the need to show it? Anything. I'll give you anything. Just please, please, cover your ass."

She flipped through more pages and checked her watch. The plane bumped through the air as if it had a flat tire until it smoothed itself out again. There was only so much drinking and eating and movie watching and magazine reading she could do. Just as the mechanical plane in front of her indicated, they were still five hours from Paris. The plane dipped and dipped again. Other passengers stirred and looked at the flight attendant for cues, but Valarie was not fazed. She had gotten so used to the turbulence throughout the years that she made it normal. Because it was. When she landed, when she felt ground underneath her, she would text her daughter, and take in the best of what was between them. If they could just get through these years, to when Jess was older, to when Jess understood what she was trying to do for her, if they could put the past behind them, just be two women together, not a teenager and a woman, if they could do that, then there would come a day when neither one of them would hardly remember what was the problem in the first place.

THE STORY OF BIDDY MASON

Some people come from greatness and mistake it for something else. If you are a baby boy named Henry Edward Huntington, born in Oneonta, for instance, a mere village in
Otsego County, in Central New York, in the year 1850, you are
unaware that your people come from what some people called
good stock. When America was revolutionizing, your people were
there. After America put its foot down, drew a line in the sand,
demanded its freedom, your people were there, at Yale, in court-
houses overseeing justice, at Harvard, your people were there.
Two of your people were *there*, in the Continental Congress. Benjamin Huntington at first. And then another. Samuel Huntington.
Chief justice of the supreme court of Connecticut. Governor of
Connecticut. But before that, another Huntington. Waiting for
that attention hog, John Hancock, to hurry up and sign his name,
waiting for the ink to dry on that overcompensating, shout-my-
name-in-the-streets signature, in 1776, so he, Samuel Huntington,
could sign his name so modestly you can hardly see it, it's so
camouflaged, surrounded by the sweeping tails and curlicues and
figure-eight flourishes of alphabets that spell the name of men who

mean to say for those who don't know: We were here. We. Were. Here. This is our declaration.

But Samuel. You have to look very hard to see him, he who signed his name Sam, not even Samuel, but Sam, just a regular Joe you would think an okay guy who's not too big for his britches, no, not him or that other Sam, Sam Adams. They're just two Sams, the kind of guys who might pour you an ale or two.

Sam Huntington, he did all that in his sixty-five years, and then he was gone. No college education, even. But who needs an education when the promise of life, for you, a Huntington, for you, a Hancock, for you, an Adams, is like standing in front of a gate, the chains cut and the obstructions thrown open to see infinity?

If you are Henry Edwards Huntington, staring through those gates thrown wide open, it's scary, all that modesty, humility, and power. How to figure out his life? What a tough road ahead.

In the meantime, he loves stories. Imagination. He has one, undervalued as they are. He loves stories so much that he collects books that tell stories in the form of history and fiction and poetry. He loves books and art and botanicals so much that one day he will collect them and give them to his city, his savior, Los Angeles. Countless books, so much art. He will acquire *major* pieces of art. One big coup is *The Blue Boy*, which pissed off the British. The London *Daily Mirror* egged him on. Who did he think he was? In 1916, some gossip columnist wrote, "I hear that Mr. H. E. Huntington, famous American millionaire, has the finest collection of the English School of pictures in the world." The columnist continued, winding up her middle finger, "He has not got the Duke of Westminster's great Gainsborough, *The Blue Boy*, though the Duke has refused an offer of eighty thousand pounds. I hope," the columnist said, sticking out her tongue, "that picture will never leave England."

Yeah. Well. Guess who was broke in 1921? The Duke took Huntington's six hundred thousand dollars like a man counting cash at the racetrack trying to make it to payday. He even threw in another Gainsborough and a Reynolds to sweeten the deal. England was so over Huntington, the greedy American. The National Gallery in London showed the painting for weeks before it was to be absconded with by a mogul. "Good-Bye to the Blue Boy" the papers said. "The Lost Masterpiece," they cried, and they blew kisses to their boy, who was going to be in some library in what one paper called "the land of freaks and freedom." This is what Huntington gives to the city. Stories and art. He changes Southern California, expands it, brings big business, opens it up, so Angelinos can get to entirely other worlds in their own city and state. Just pick a train track. Still, in 1921, the *Los Angeles Herald Examiner* understood the big deal about a story. The material benefits are cool, the paper says, and trains. We wouldn't be anywhere without trains, but compared to a library? Not even close. The paper called the Huntington Library a "mass of books." The paper said that, "from its mass of books will be created new thoughts, new knowledge, and thought as the one imperishable, ever productive effort of mankind."

One thing about libraries, though, is that even they can't contain all the stories, and Huntington, himself, only collected books "of interest to him."

The man who loved stories is usually the story of Los Angeles. Those Mulhollands, those Chandlers, those Dohenys. They are always the story.

But before this, before he is Huntington Beach, Huntington Library, Mr. Pacific Electric, overseeing the tracks being laid into the ground like steel veins that will pump the people in and around and throughout the city, he was lost. What to do with his life? What to do? He was, what we call now, a screwup, the way his uncle Collis saw it. A more generous way of putting it is that it took him a few tries and help from his father Solon and his uncle Collis, who supplied the dough, gave him jobs, even handed him a logging business

to oversee, which he screwed up. He tried. He really did, and sometimes he succeeded. In West Virginia, he bragged about his successes
in a letter home to Mom, blowing on his fingernails and buffing them
on his lapels. "We had a flood on the Coal River," he wrote. "I had
most excellent luck with my timber, as I had six or seven thousand
dollars worth of timber in the river, and did not lose a single log!"

But sometimes, guys like that, they think they hit a triple when
they were born on third base. When Uncle Collis takes the training
wheels off and gives him half an interest in the company and the
other half is bought by Collis's chief resident lobbyist in Washington
for *his* kid, another third-baser named Franchot, boy did they make
a mess. These kids didn't know what they were doing. Huntington
kept hitting Collis up for loans, until Collis finally held up his palm
and shook his head with finality. That other rich kid, Franchot, who
liked a sip now and then, was embarrassed that he had to sell his
Wells Fargo stock so they could stay afloat. Well, the elder Franchot and Collis had had enough. Pulled the plug. Franchot, Civil
War *General* Franchot, before he was a Washington lobbyist with
money floating out of his pockets as he walked down the street,
told Collis he was through with the young knuckleheads. "All of
this is mortifying to me and annoys me," he said. "I think it is a
piece of boys play. Nonsensical and simply shows that they are not
equal to the business. I am disgusted with such damned foolishness.
I think they should both be spanked into manly habits."

But to be fair, a lot of this is on General Franchot and Uncle Collis.
Years before this, Huntington wanted to take a job—any job—and
his uncle told him to wait. "But I found a job," Huntington said, anxious to get started with his life. He was a porter, moving heavy stuff
all around the place, doing hard labor like somebody who had no
choice. Uncle Collis was not amused. Huntington was proud of his
three bucks a week and thought he could get even more "on account
of having the good will of Uncle Collis." But Uncle Collis, one of the

four big men who they say built the Southern Pacific Railroad, had an idea about what the Huntingtons were worth. Those three dollars a week? Those three dollars weren't worth the paper they were printed on. "It would be better," Collis said, "to accept no salary at all than to take three dollars a week." To have a Huntington work for free was to make a point. The point of working for free was a declaration: We don't *have* to work. Three dollars is beneath us. If we own everything, can be anything, can do anything, that three dollars? It's already yours. Don't be a dummy. Think like a tycoon.

So, how is it Huntington's fault that he and the Franchot kid didn't know what they were doing?

But he's got a cushion. That cushion buys time. He learns. He makes his own money, gets the hang of things, Huntington. But California calls him, makes him truly the man his uncle always thought he could be. He had to leave New York and come west. Of course. He did what so many before and after him did: make himself, his name, his story, way out West, in California. Los Angeles, California, she opened her arms wide, rebirthed him, pulled him to her breast, and nourished him. He nestled against her and admitted to the world, after all was said and done, that he would be nothing without her.

In California, he is far from the boy in Oneonta, asking for a bit to tide him over. He's the *dude*. In Santa Cruz, the newspaper is giddy about him. He's got swag, they say, he's got "that force and breadth of character we are pleased to designate, to be an invaluable acquisition to our commonwealth." He's an executive, a big man, working alongside his uncle, and later, in 1898, in what they called friendly competition with Uncle Collis's Southern Pacific Railroad, Huntington lays it down and gives the city Red Cars on Sixth and Main Streets, coming out of a building *he* built, the largest building west of Chicago in 1905, the Huntington, it's called at first, and later the Pacific Electric Building, Red Cars spilling out to take Los Angelinos all over the city, 24/7, outside the city to suburbs, to places like a beach by the name of Huntington, already. It was a wrap. California gave birth to Huntington, the stories go, and he, the stories go, gave birth to California. Sometimes the stories say he built the city, the railroads, and oftentimes the stories state, curiously and with strange passivity, facts like "train tracks were laid." The rest, they tell us, again and again until we believe it, is history.

But when they say that he built buildings, we know that he didn't roll up his sleeves and lay bricks right there, his trousers dusted up and ruined by concrete. So much of the story is missing. Who laid the tracks with their hands? Who built the buildings with their hands? Look to the newspapers, then, carrying on about the Chinese immigration, labor unions blaming them for taking jobs and lowering wages. That's one of the oldest stories. A fairytale that gets told a lot. It's an oldie but a goodie. Huntington said it though, somewhere, if you look for it. "I couldn't have built my railroad without them."

Wait a minute. The newspapers were for news and all, but not that kind of news. There were facts that were more interesting. They loved Huntington for all he did for the state and the city, and for certain antics, like when Huntington takes his swag and friendly competition to the next level and marries Uncle Collis's widow, his own aunt. The papers usually love the guy, but they mess with him about this, as if to say, *We know this is California and all, where the rules are fast and loose, but come on.* The papers say:

**MARRIAGE MIXES UP RELATIONSHIP
OF HUNTINGTON**

HE BECOMES:

His Own Uncle.

Nephew of His Wife.

Brother-in-Law of His Mother-in-Law.

Great Uncle of His Own Children.

It's a good laugh, the scandal of it all, but these papers seem to not know the half. American lineage is way more complicated than that. A nephew marrying his aunt? Amateur hour.

HERE'S ANOTHER STORY, A good one for a man like Huntington, who loved them so much, depending. Before tracks "were laid," before Huntington was born, in 1848, Biddy Mason walked 1,700 miles west behind a 300-wagon caravan, all the way from Mississippi, stopping in Utah for three years or so, before finally setting foot in San Bernardino with her master and 150 wagons. Two years before Huntington was born, seventy-two years after his relative put his timid or humble signature on a document that declared it self-evident that all men were created equal, well, of course, the devil was in the details. All those important men in the room, with their signatures on paper, so much brilliance and vision—and blindness. Men. Biddy didn't know it as she walked behind oxen, avoiding the piles they dropped, because for now, they were only on their way to Utah, but in California that one word, *men*, would open the gate that confused young Huntington, it was so gaping and yawning wide. Biddy, though, she would know exactly what to do once she came upon the unfathomable thing called *choice*.

First, though, she walked. She took her first step behind the wagon caravan, thinking about all the things she would have to do along the way. She would have to deliver all the babies that would be born, across the plains, in the desert. She would have to herd the oxen and cook the meals, set up and break down camp. Plus, she had her own little ones, all daughters, ten and four, and the new one, who had only been in the world for months and would not remember what it was like to be a slave. She would have to take care of them, but not as well as she would take care of all the others in the caravan. Master Smith had placed his hand on her shoulder, and it had felt too warm, as the sun was already a blaze in the dewy morning. He told her all the things she knew already. "You ready for this journey, Biddy? It will be a long one. See to it that you care for Mistress Smith above all." Because he was called by God, because he believed in the Mormon Church, they were going west.

She took one step, and then another. Another, another. One thousand and seven hundred miles to go. Biddy kept walking because no such a thing as stopping existed. The creamy red soil of Mississippi coated the bottom of her shoes—when she wore them—and also covered the pads of her feet, when her shoes pained her enough to take them off and she just wanted to feel the ground beneath her. Stopping. The man who owned her wouldn't allow it. So she walked and walked. In Arkansas, she brought life into the world, delivering one baby boy, the son of another new Mormon convert, a young woman of sixteen, who nearly died. When she wasn't walking, and cooking, and herding oxen, she nursed that baby, her milk infusing his tiny body with proteins, fats, and vitamins that would be the beginning of him growing hard bones and muscle and heart, growing up to be a tall, strong man. But for now, newly born, his blue blind eyes looked into the face of Biddy, into something he would never be able to see for all of his life on earth. Biddy could not remember the last time that her own child, with pale skin and loose sandy curls like her sisters, the sisters that the slaves all thought were the picture of Master Smith, had drank her mother's milk.

There was dying. She could lie down and die, die in the golden field of South Dakota, her fading brown eyes staring up at the sky, her substitute ocean for the one she had never seen, not the one her heart and memory told her about. That one, somehow, she had seen. Somewhere in the lives before her own she saw that ocean. And so she put one foot in front of the other, then the other, and another, for minutes and hours and days and weeks and months and years, until there was the very first step onto, and into, California.

The soil in California was not the same as the soil in Mississippi. In Mississippi, the soil stuck to Biddy and left its rusty hue on her skin even when she brushed it off. Clay. The soil was clay, and it clung to her toes as if it were trying to reshape the bones in her feet. But California's soil was different. The dry soil in San Bernardino dusted Biddy's skin lightly, like talcum powder. When she brushed if off, the soil left a hint of itself, but when she rubbed it into her arm, it disappeared, and Biddy could not tell whether she was looking at the earth or at her skin.

The caravan had disembarked. The settlers were getting out of their wagons and stretching their legs, their arms, their backs. The sun and wind had weathered the canvas cover of Master Smith's wagon, and Biddy saw that she would have to patch it once they got settled. It had been a long, long journey. "We have made it, Biddy," her Master Smith said. He took off his hat and wiped his brow with his wrist and smoothed his black hair back before putting his hat on again. He climbed down from the wagon and helped his wife down, scooping her up when she leaned her slight body out of the wagon. He placed her onto California gently, the first time her feet had ever touched the state.

Biddy said nothing. She stood, favoring her left foot, as her right foot had blisters on top of blisters, and something else wrong that Biddy could not figure. This right foot would not be able to hold her weight for the rest of her life. Her daughters stood on either side of her, the oldest holding the hand of her baby sister, who was prattling on and on, telling them all a story about the future. That sister would have a daughter, who would have a daughter who would have a son who looked like his father. He and his family would be Los Angelinos, would call themselves white and be lost to their original mother forever. Now, though, Biddy shaded her eyes with her hands. The sun was insisting that it was much more spectacular than the ground on which they stood. She pointed to the San Gabriel Mountains with the other hand, watercolors of lavender and yellow and red. "Look," Biddy said to her children. "Look at that. Ain't that a picture."

Those mountains were a sign. Walking through Oklahoma, Biddy had met two free black people, Charles and Elizabeth, and they told her: In California, nobody owns nobody. "When you get there?" Elizabeth had said, rubbing the nose of a caravan ox dripping with sweat, "be sure to find you somebody that knows what all he's doing." She had strange green eyes that sat in the dark brown velvet of her face like jewels on display in a case. And Elizabeth's husband, Charles, had locked eyes with Biddy. "Listen what she telling you. There's going to be some peoples that are going to know how to do what you need done." He had pulled on his long beard and walked away with Elizabeth, never to be seen by Biddy again.

Brigham Young had warned Smith. In doing the Lord's work, one had to be careful. "Do not take your slaves to California," he had said. "Establish our Mormon community, but do it elsewhere." Smith didn't listen. Biddy was his property. She had been a gift. A wedding gift to Smith and his wife. How could California have any say in those facts?

Therefore, Biddy worked for free, for almost five more years, the only way she had ever worked for thirty-seven years.

Biddy's daughter was in love, in 1856. A boy by the name of Owens was the man she wanted. That was the beginning of choices. He was free. His parents were free, and they were the kind of people who would tell the seventeen-year-old and her mother how to do what they needed done. These free black people in California, they were not afraid to walk into a courtroom and remind judges and courts and government of all things self-evident. When Biddy tried to explain to Smith that she would like to be free, was in fact already free, and that he was breaking the law, he packed up his three wagons and demanded that Biddy, her daughters, and all of his slaves get behind them. They would leave for Texas, where things made sense to him and where God would be waiting to deliver redemption to all Mormons.

So Biddy got behind the wagons. They got as far as Cajon Pass before a posse enforced the law. Because Biddy's daughter was in love with a man who was free, he alerted the Sheriff of Los Angeles County, this strange place where black people could get white people into trouble. These cowboys and vaqueros who made up the posse were not the same as the overseers in Mississippi. They seemed to put ideas about a place above ideas about people. This was West, and whatever went on in some other place, in some other time, before Smith and his slaves got here, was over. In three days Judge Benjamin Hayes, sweating under a heavy black robe because of the desert heat, said it was so. One need only look at the constitution—California's constitution—and one would not find the devil hiding and shifting shape behind, and in between, the black ink of the letters.

What does one do when one is a wedding gift in one lifetime, and in that lifetime never could have fathomed a life beyond that binding bridal ribbon? After thirty-seven years, Biddy knew as she walked out of the courthouse. She would work, and get paid to work, and every coin, every piece of paper that counted as money, she would save. She worked as a nurse. She worked as a midwife, her hands on hundreds of babies all over Los Angeles, catching them as they slid out of their mothers or pulling them out gently when they were undecided about this world. She got paid to deliver the babies, and she did not have to feed them with the milk of her body. She got paid, and no amount of money was too little. The money that she touched with her calloused hands was hard to let go of and so she didn't spend it, because she had everything she wanted. Her body.

She got paid, and the money that passed through her fingers, money marked with the oil of her body and the traces of skin from the babies she delivered and the people she nursed and stroked on their way to the hereafter, that money went into Los Angeles. It took her ten years to save $250. With $250, she bought land, the woman who was once a wedding present, right in the middle of Downtown Los Angeles, on Spring Street. She became a businesswoman, an entrepreneur, gave to charities, built schools, fed and housed the people in her city. She visited prisoners, telling them that they were in prison, yes, but one fine day, they could find a way to be free. She founded an elementary school for black children and helped found a travelers-aid center for people who were traveling, those women and children who might get stranded, be taken advantage of, exploited. Most travelers-aid societies worried about white slavery, but Biddy had a feeling of being stranded in Mississippi, all the way to California, every step of those 1,700 miles.

In years and years, California will be so dry that people all over the country will know about it, shake their heads, and be glad they don't live there. But then, when Biddy lived in Los Angeles, there were floods every spring, floods that destroyed dozens and dozens of people's homes. What could a person do? They called what she did a word that Biddy didn't know. They called it *philanthropy*. But back home, in Mississippi, Biddy and the other slaves called it taking care of your people.

She knew this: Some people in Los Angeles didn't have homes. And they were hungry. One rainy day, boots caked with mud, the bottom of her skirt heavy with water, Biddy walks into a grocery on Fourth and Spring to do the only thing there is to do: She pays the man who owns the store to feed all the folks who need it.

She looks around the store, smells the sharp tangy cheese wrapped in cloth, stares at the cans neatly arranged on the shelf behind the storekeeper, tomatoes and corn and string beans and loganberries wrapped in brilliant colors like prizes.

"I don't expect you to give away food," Biddy says. The storekeeper, O'Malley, nods, just once, in punctuated agreement, and twists the red handlebar of his moustache. Everybody knows that Biddy is fair, but everybody also knows that saying no to Auntie Mason or Grandma Mason, as the people call her, is a powerfully difficult thing.

On a balmy evening in 1872, Biddy dines with Pío de Jesús Pico, eighteen years her senior. He is first-generation Californio, a descendant of Los Pobladores, two of forty-four people who, in 1781, came to California and created El Pueblo de Nuestra Señora la Reina de los Ángeles del Río de Porciúncula. Twenty-six of Los Pobladores have African ancestors, and Pío is the son of people who have Africa in their blood. Pío and Biddy, they have marveled at this in the past, the fact that they share the same mother, Africa, and that they could find themselves, so far from home, in the only other place that could possibly be their home. They dine at his lavish thirty-three-room hotel, Casa de Pico, on lamb and corn and rice with beans. They talk business under gaslit chandeliers, Biddy lounging comfortably on Pío's carved rosewood furniture. Sometimes they speak in English and sometimes in Spanish, which Biddy has learned to speak fluently. This is what people will do, speak both, until El Pueblo de Nuestra Señora la Reina de los Ángeles del Río de Porciúncula becomes Los Angeles, until Calle Principal becomes Main Street, until one day people won't be able to understand the mockery of a bumptious idea called "English Only."

Pío and Biddy, they discuss the news of the day, according to the newspaper, *La Estrella de Los Angeles*, which reports all things in Spanish and English, two pages for each. There are terrible things that the newspaper reports, such as every hanging and whipping of men who are lawless, and there is good news for Pío, which is that whiskey is fifty cents a quart, a manageable price to keep his hotel stocked and his guests pleased. Before this, he was governor of Mexican California, before it became the thirty-first state, when it was a mere territory and then a sovereignty. He will be a rich man, for a time, and then lose it all. But for now, he takes care not to drop a single morsel on his suit and tie.

"I hear, Biddy, that you are thinking of a church," he says. The medals and decorations pinned to his suit jingle lightly as he cuts his lamb. He points his fork at her and winks, and Biddy is amazed, once again, how very small Los Angeles is. It is easy to know just about everything about everybody.

"Sí," Biddy says. "Quiero comenzar una iglesia para la gente negra. Para la gente negra, pero cada uno será bienvenido." She wants the church badly, a church for black people, but wants to make sure that no one will stand at the threshold, afraid to put one foot in front of the other and walk in. She has made a fortune in California, not working for free, and now she is worth three hundred thousand dollars. But a church. With all the things she has done with her life, this is the thing she wants most now.

"Bien entonces," Pío says. "Usted debería tener su iglesia. I'll come," he says. "I will be one of the first." And both he and Biddy laugh, because Pío's expensive tastes and extravagant life are not all he is known for. Pío likes his gambling, the people of Los Angeles say.

Biddy did not tell Pío that evening why she must erect a church. Someday, she decided, she would tell him, the whole story from beginning to end. It was difficult to say, though, in English or in Spanish, how she felt, living in Los Angeles. It came to her in flashes, the thing that was difficult to say. It came to her on her way to Pío's. Walking down Main Street that gray day in 1871, the ground was soft from a light rain earlier, and her boots left her tracks in the road. A boy she had delivered ran right into her, nearly knocked the cake she was taking to Pío out of her arms. "Where you going, son?" she had said, holding onto his shoulder tight with her one free hand. He had stood up straight and still. "I'm sorry, Grandma Mason. I'm sorry, ma'am."

"In such a hurry. Only me and you out here on the street, and you running into folks like somebody done got after you. Where you going, son?"

"Nowhere, ma'am," the boy said, pulling on the collar of his shirt. "I just like to run." She had delivered this boy not eight years ago. He almost didn't make it. He was one of those babies that didn't care if he was coming or going, either way. He was half in and half out of this world, and Biddy had to bribe him with the gentle touch of her hands, had to massage his chest. That was when he opened his mouth wide and told everybody he was there to stay.

"All right then," Biddy said. She held his face in her hand. He was looking just like his father's picture, Oscar De la Court, those same gold eyes and tight curls framing his face like lace. She let him go and watched him pick up where he left off, sprinting down Calle Principal for no reason except to do it.

This had made her think of church, to put words to the story she could not exactly tell. Something about a miracle. How was it possible that she was walking down the street, her own person, in her own place, with money enough, with the hands to bring a dying boy into the world, when just yesterday she was endlessly walking behind oxen? She didn't know how to say what she felt, except what she felt was church. Some called it luck, some called it hard work, some called it greatness, but Biddy called it God. *There is no way*, she often thought, *no way I did all of this by myself.* The only explanation was God, so Biddy gave Los Angeles its First African Methodist Episcopal church in 1872, where she worshipped and talked about miracles until 1890, until she was gone.

For a very long time, people mourned the death of Biddy Mason. They missed her. They loved her. They did not know how

Los Angeles could function without her. And all the people she touched in some way, her invisible handprint on their lives, they died or they lived and gave life to others, and years went by, inevitably, years and years, so the story of Biddy Mason and the people who knew it vanished, became invisible, like the air we breathe.

TIMES CHANGED. EL PUEBLO de Nuestra Señora la Reina de los Ángeles del Río de Porciúncula became Los Angeles, and then Los Angeles became L.A., when even Los Angeles was too much for some mouths. Los Pobladores started it all, and then other men got credit for making the city what it is, which is always hard to say, since Los Angeles is many things to many people. Huntington, his trains made Downtown Los Angeles a destination and, also, a place you can get away from, thank God. Go to the beach or someplace far away. But the cars. The cars come in, and nobody loves a car like a Los Angelino. Don't touch their steering wheels. Out of their cold dead hands! So Huntington's red train cars vanish. You can't even see where the tracks used to be. It's all covered up and gone. Downtown, being conquered and left behind like a pretty dame in a Raymond Chandler novel who gave it up too easily, becomes a ghost town, deserted, newspapers rolling and twisting down the street like the tumbleweeds that passed Biddy Mason as she walked through California.

And then, times change, once more. Downtown is revitalized. The early pioneers, they were broke like the early, early pioneers, who came to California in their wagons out of desperation or some kind of calling. Those early Downtowners were too broke for the Westside, and were even too broke for Silver Lake or Echo Park. Or maybe they weren't broke. Maybe they were just that weird kind of people who like sidewalks and brick and skyline. But those second-wave pioneers. They gentrified with a vengeance, entitlement blazing like guns, driving their shiny BMWs with enough horse power to get them anywhere they want to go fast, wasted as that power is, since being stuck on the 110 or the 101, trying to get home during rush hour, that horsepower will only get them about a mile every half hour.

Your friend is one of them. She calls you and asks you to come down from Riverside. Hang out. Get out of the Inland Empire. "Get out of the I.E.," she says. "Come hang."

But you don't know. "Driving into Downtown on a Friday night? From Riverside? It's kind of a schlep. It'll take forever if I don't leave, like, hours before I need to. And the parking. Unbelievable."

"You haven't heard of the miracle of rapid transportation?" your friend says. "The train. Take the train."

And so you do, you take the train all the way from Riverside, and then, when you get to Union Station, you take the Red Line to Downtown, to Pershing Square, which, to your untrained eye, is a straight-up freak show. When you emerge from the cave of the platform, the escalator taking you up and up into the shadowy day-light, the people make you nervous. Some are arguing with the air around them. Some are arguing with the sky. Some are slipping drugs into each other's hands. A man with no teeth and no shirt and no shoes screams at you, "Just a quarter! Goddamn!" You have your earbuds in, so you pretend not to hear. You look around, for anybody that seems, well, not homeless. You walk as fast as you can to Pacific Electric Lofts and call your friend, tell her to hurry the hell up and meet you in the lobby, where you look at the black-and-white photos of the Red Cars, which you look at every time you come.

Your friend wants to take you to the latest place to eat. It's so good, she says, you have to stand around and wait for a table. You roll your eyes, because you are not the kind of person who thinks that's the litmus test for food worth eating. Food should not be something that anybody has to wait for. But you're a visitor. She knows better than you.

It's an Italian place, Maccheroni Republic, it's called, on Spring, between Third and Fourth. After she hands you a bottle of water, one for her and one for you (How can it be 105 degrees in October?), the two of you start down Main Street, which you will never be able to imagine as a wide dirt road, near deserted, horses tied up on their posts. There's just way too much going on for that. It's rush hour, so the cars fill every lane in the one-way street, honking and idling with loud rumbles. And you have to be careful crossing the street on Sixth—if you don't look over your left shoulder after the light turns green, some asshole will run you down. The pedestrian never, ever has the right of way, no matter what anybody says. Sure, the pedestrian can be right—dead right. "Not too long ago," your friend says, "somebody got ran over on the corner of Olympic and Ninth."

And you say, "I don't know why you chose to live here."

This time, you cross without a near-death experience. No guarantees about the next. Your friend has almost gotten hit, like, ten times, she says. Just walking, crossing on a green light. "They don't even see me," she says. "I've just been lucky, I swear."

Walking down Main, it's hard for you to tell potential danger from good-natured people having fun. Brothers on the corner in front of Hotel Leonide, in front of the Sanborn Hotel, play their music, some O'Jays, and say, "Right, right, how you all doin this evening?" "Hey, my lovely sistas!" another man shouts, the beer in his hand held high in the sky. But the next minute, somebody is being blessed out like it's a sport. "Motherfucker, I know you better pay me, your damn ass. Not tonight, not tomorrow, but right now." You take your cues from your friend, like a passenger on a plane watching a flight attendant during turbulence. If something's about to pop off, she'll let you know.

But the more you walk, the more you relax. The sun is going down, and in the distance you can see mountains, mountains that seem to end right on the corner of Main and Cesar Chavez, just past where Biddy and Pío had dinner one humid evening in 1871. You don't know that. You are just taken with the picture in front of you. When you look down the street, the buildings on either side seem to form a long passageway, a corridor that leads you to sierra that looks as though it can be rolled away once the sun goes down, put away on the back lot of a movie set, and brought back to be spectacular, again, tomorrow. The sky, turning purple, fading to blue and then black, is lit like a carnival. The neon of the Rosslyn Lofts does that, red and yellow and blue and green lights shout ROSSLYN HOTEL, not looking classy, like it must have, back in 1914, but calling to mind, instead, a working girl wearing yellow shoes and blue eye shadow and a red dress with green sequins on top because she doesn't know any better. The roof of the annex across the street would like to shout NEW MILLION DOLLAR HOTEL ROSSLYN, but that neon has not been lit for years. In 1914, a million dollars built the Rosslyn, the largest hotel on the Pacific Coast, and boy was it grand, beaux-art grand. There's a neon heart, too, because the Heart brothers built it—had the money to build it—but you and your friend, you don't really know about that. You just think it's pretty damn cool to look at. As much as you'll take Riverside over Downtown any day of the week, you have never even tried to pretend that that building, burned-out neon and all, was not the bomb. Pío would have agreed. He would die a poor man in 1894, would never live to see its 1914 opening, its 1,100 rooms, but he would have thought the building, in its day, most grand, a worthy competitor to his own Pico House. Biddy, a woman who was not show-offy, would have thought, perhaps, that the neon gilded the lily, but she would have approved that Los Angeles had tried, in some small way, to take care of its people by renting some of those rooms to folks with empty pockets.

You get to the corner of Main and Fifth. On your right is a place that used to be called Pete's but is now called Ledlow and will be called something else five or ten or a hundred years from now. Your friend, she misses the old Pete's. "It had style," she says. "History. This new place, I'm sure it's all right, but look at it." She gestures and shakes her head, as if pointing to a scene of an accident. "It's all white. White walls, white floors, white lights. I can't go in there," she says. "I just can't. I'll feel like I'm going to the gynecologist for a Pap smear." To you, though, why even fight change? Nobody can do anything about it. Nothing stays the same. On some street, somewhere, is a building looking at its future, looking across the street at a parking lot, the ghost of a structure that was there for a hundred years before it was torn down.

On Spring, you make a left at a courtyard, Broadway Spring Center, a shortcut to the restaurant. You pass a Wells Fargo and a dry cleaner's. You pass a concrete wall, some kind of art installation or something. Your friend pauses, but you say, "I'm starving. I am literally starving. Let's go." You blow past some other kind of sculpture, poles and what looks like pistons that are supposed to have water flowing out of them, but most of them are dry, look like they have been dry for years, and a few of them just have trickles of water halfheartedly crawling to the ground. You're so hungry, but there's a line, more like a crowd, at Maccheroni Republic. Half an hour wait, at least.

"Now what?" you say. Your friend shrugs. "Let's go look at that wall."

So you do. You walk back to it, stand in front of it, reading it silently. The wall tells you a story, going right to left, but you are reading it out of order. The wall tells you all kinds of things that nobody has ever told you. Stories you didn't even know existed, stories like the pueblo of Los Angeles was established in 1781, that the first settlers, from Mexico, had African ancestors, that someone named Biddy Mason delivered hundreds of babies, that Biddy saved $250 and bought land, one of the first blacks to be able to, that she was a slave and then she wasn't, that she walked all the way to California from Mississippi.

"No way," you say. "That's bogus that she walked here all the way from Mississippi. Who does that?"

"Nobody—now," your friend says, "but she was a slave. I bet you walking from Mississippi was the least of it."

"No way," you say, shaking your head.

Your friend touches the wall, a piece of marble that replicates Biddy Mason's court-ordered freedom. "What then? She caught a cab? Flew? Took a train? Even I know they didn't start the railroad until 1863."

"But that's only because you live in that building you live in, that you know about trains. Nobody else knows that kind of crap."

Your friend agrees with you, because she says nothing. You just stare at the wall, trying to read pictures of documents carved into stone.

There are fifteen more minutes before your names will be called. Your names. Who is going to know them? A man hobbles up to you dragging a big bag full of plastic. He holds out his dark brown hand, silent. He doesn't even have to ask. Money. You both shake your head, but you give him your empty plastic bottles, since he's collecting them.

Later, at the restaurant, you pull out your phones and pull up all kinds of facts, now that you know they are out there. Of course they have always been out there, these facts, these stories. You have just never quite thought about them. The artist is named on Wikipedia; somebody named Sheila Levrant de Bretteville has blown your mind. You and your friend, you read each other facts about

Biddy, about Los Pobladores, and you will never think of Los Angeles in the same way again.

On the train back to Riverside, you will even think about the man with the bag full of plastic, for some reason. All the people like him on the streets. Why don't they do something? But that question is too big. So you ask yourself another question. The question is this: Who is he, the man with a bag full of plastic? You wonder. Where did he come from? How do you get to be a man dragging a bag of plastic around? Some stories you will never be able to find in all the libraries of the world put together. This man's story, it's just not going to be there. He doesn't have the money to put his name on a building or a stretch of beach.

But it's no less a miracle, what nobody knows about him, what you will never know, and it's no less true: He is the son of the son of the son of the son of a man who knew Biddy Mason. It's true. He is the son of the son of the son of the son of a man who worked for free, just like Biddy. For free, that original son built America with his bare hands and with his knees in the dirt so other men could have money to build buildings and hire other people to lay train tracks. Biddy stood right where that man with the plastic bag was standing when you and your friend left him. She was wearing white gloves, and her dress was fine, and she was on her way home to take off that finery.

She had been called, yet again, to deliver you into your future.

ACKNOWLEDGMENTS

I WOULD LIKE TO thank everyone at Counterpoint, especially my editor, Dan Smetanka, for his investment in my work and for his enthusiasm about these stories in particular. A deep thanks to my agent, Jennifer Lyons, whose faith in my work has led me to great places, and to the very generous and kind Lorin Stein at the *Paris Review*, whose judicious edits of "She Deserves Everything She Gets" were invaluable.

I'm ever grateful to Victoria Patterson, Danzy Senna, and Sarah Shun-lien Bynum, who are the best readers and whip crackers, and whose writing motivates me to be uncompromising. To Gordon Davis and Bruce Smith, who read early drafts of "The Story of Biddy Mason": Thank you.

Thanks to Barrett Briske for her sharp and discerning copyedits, Kelly Winton for her cover design, and Joe Goodale for his sharp-eyed proofread.

Special thanks to Sabrina "Magic Fingers" Williams for crossing the "T"s and dotting the "I"s and to Carolie Dominick-Mitchell for her research assistance. Eternal thanks to Kerry Brian Ingram, for everything.

CREDITS

"Rogues" appeard in the *Indiana Review*, Summer, 2009

"Sunshine" appeared as "Threesome" in *The Dictionary of Failed Relationships*, December 2007

"Now, in the Not Quite Dark" appeared in *Rattling Wall*, December 2013

"Because That's Just Easier" appeared in the *Southern California Review*, 2014

"No Blaming the Harvard Boys" appeared in *Huizache: The Magazine of Latino Literature*, Fall 2014

"Buildings Talk" appeared in *Watchlist: 32 Short Stories by Persons of Interest*, 2015

"Art is Always and Everywhere the Secret Confessor" appeared in *Hello LA: The Grove Issue*, Airbnb and McSweeny's, 2013

"The Liberace Museum" appeared in *Ninth Letter*, 2005

"She Deserves Everything She Gets" appeared in the *Paris Review*, Spring 2016

Ellie Partovi

ABOUT THE AUTHOR

DANA JOHNSON is the author of *Break Any Woman Down*, winner of the Flannery O'Connor Award for Short Fiction, and the novel *Elsewhere, California*. Both books were nominees for the Hurston/Wright Legacy Award. Born and raised in and around Los Angeles, she is a professor of English at the University of Southern California. Learn more at www.danajohnsonauthor.com.